Congratulations on your new job!!

Love Greg & Pat

STORIES *Baby Khaki's Wings*

Anar Ali

VIKING
CANADA

VIKING CANADA

Published by the Penguin Group

Penguin Group (Canada), 90 Eglinton Avenue East, Suite 700, Toronto, Ontario, Canada M4P 2Y3
(a division of Pearson Penguin Canada Inc.)

Penguin Group (USA) Inc., 375 Hudson Street, New York, New York 10014, U.S.A.
Penguin Books Ltd, 80 Strand, London WC2R 0RL, England
Penguin Ireland, 25 St Stephen's Green, Dublin 2, Ireland (a division of Penguin Books Ltd)
Penguin Group (Australia), 250 Camberwell Road, Camberwell, Victoria 3124, Australia
(a division of Pearson Australia Group Pty Ltd)
Penguin Books India Pvt Ltd, 11 Community Centre, Panchsheel Park, New Delhi – 110 017, India
Penguin Group (NZ), cnr Airborne and Rosedale Roads, Albany, Auckland 1310, New Zealand
(a division of Pearson New Zealand Ltd)
Penguin Books (South Africa) (Pty) Ltd, 24 Sturdee Avenue, Rosebank, Johannesburg 2196,
South Africa

Penguin Books Ltd, Registered Offices: 80 Strand, London WC2R 0RL, England

First published 2006

1 2 3 4 5 6 7 8 9 10 (FR)

Copyright © Anar Ali, 2006

In "The Weight of Pearls" on pages 26–27, the speech of the Imam is reprinted with permission
from *Aga Khan III: Selected Speeches and Writings* by K.K. Aziz, Kegan Paul International, 1988.

*We acknowledge the support of the Canada Council for the Arts which last
year invested $21.7 million in writing and publishing throughout Canada.*

*Nous remercions de son soutien le Conseil des Arts du Canada, qui a investi
21,7 millions de dollars l'an dernier dans les lettres et l'édition à travers le Canada.*

Manufactured in Canada.

ISBN 0-670-06425-4

Library and Archives Canada Cataloguing in Publication data available upon request.

Visit the Penguin Group (Canada) website at **www.penguin.ca**

Special and corporate bulk purchase rates available; please see
www.penguin.ca/corporatesales or call 1-800-399-6858, ext. 477 or 474

For my parents
Nurali and Rozina Mohamedali

Speak—your lips are free.
Speak—this tongue is still yours.
This magnificent body is still yours.
Speak—your life is still yours.

—from "Speak" by Faiz Ahmed Faiz
  (translated by Daud Kamal)

STORIES

The Weight of Pearls

Due to the war, the community had to wait years upon years before they could physically see their Imam again and properly celebrate his Diamond Jubilee. When the war ended in 1945, they anxiously waited for word. A full year later, a telegram with the news finally arrived! The community in Tanganyika could not believe their good fortune—the Imam had chosen only two places in the entire world, Bombay and Dar es Salaam, to celebrate the sixty years of his benevolent rule as spiritual father. The Diamond Jubilee celebrations would give them a chance to mark his leadership by weighing him against diamonds.

As soon as they received the auspicious news, the community in Dar es Salaam broke out in grand celebrations with nightly programs of *dandia-raas* and food in the courtyard of the jamatkhana. The entire R.K. Jiwa family joined the celebrations: Mr. and Mrs. Jiwa, their second son, Nizar, all five of their daughters, both sets of grandparents, all the uncles, aunties, cousin-brothers, cousin-sisters, and so on. Only Shamshu, the eldest son of Mr. and Mrs. Jiwa, kept his distance. He preferred to watch the celebrations rather than participate because he found crowds to be overwhelming. Even as a little boy, he would recoil from the intense noise in the Jiwa household. Noise and the excesses of the outer world, in general, seemed to disturb the balance inside Shamshu's body. He preferred to find a safe corner in the house and read fairy tales and rhymes or create little stories in his head. At night, he would sometimes slip outside to stare at the sky or shine a flashlight into it hoping to create a small pin of light on the dark canvas.

Mr. and Mrs. Jiwa noticed Shamshu's oddities, but hoped (and prayed) that in time he would grow out of them. Eventually, though, they gave up hope, because even now, at the age of sixteen, he had not improved at all. Thank God I have another son, Mr. Jiwa thought. Shamshu hardly noticed his parents' disapproval; he was accustomed to not fitting in—not only at home but also at school and jamatkhana. For the most part, Shamshu didn't mind; it was only once in a while that he felt lonely, as if he were a fish in its own bowl. But no one else was interested in the same things he was, so what choice did he have? He had to be true to himself.

SHAMSHU LEANED OVER the railing from the library high above the jamatkhana courtyard and watched the celebrations below: troops of volunteers in smart grey uniforms stood behind tables stacked with trays of white cake; barrels overflowed with pink sherbet chock full of *takmaria;* gaggles of children darted through the rows of people playing *dandia* or around the women playing *raasra* who had to pull up their colourful saris when the circle turned to a frantic beat. Fascinated by the women's feet, Shamshu bent farther over the railing. Stepstepclapturnclap. The sound of the women's feet resonated with his breathing and soon, he felt as if his body was spinning like the skirt of a whirling dervish. In moments like this Shamshu was able to tune everything else so that he felt like his body, mind, and soul had been fused together—as if a scale had been re-balanced inside him, the needle coming to rest at zero, giving him a great sense of peace and calm.

Fatima Noorani, Nizar's classmate, tapped Shamshu on his shoulder. He turned in surprise.

"Your mother's looking for you." Fatima twirled the end of her ponytail around her finger.

"Huh?"

"Your mother asked me to come and get you. See." She pointed below to a woman in a peacock-blue sari.

Shamshu looked down to see his mother waving at him; she motioned for him to come down. Shamshu nodded, but he was disappointed that his thoughts had been disturbed.

Fatima pointed to the book under Shamshu's arm. "Oh, so you must be the one who keeps signing out all the Rumi?"

Shamshu didn't say anything; he was surprised by her question. It was as if he had been wading in a river when suddenly he found himself at its mouth, gushing into the ocean.

"Return it soon. I want to sign it out." Fatima pushed her glasses up the ridge of her nose with a finger.

Shamshu stretched his arm out, the book in the palm of his hand.

"No, silly. I don't mean now. Finish it first."

"It's okay. I've had it for too long."

"Okay. But why don't you take my Nasir-i Khusraw? His poetry is very beautiful too. You know this book?" Fatima held up the poet's *Divan*.

Shamshu shrugged, a little embarrassed that he hadn't even heard of this poet.

"*'The exoteric of revelation is like brackish water, but the esoteric like pearls for the wise. Pearls and jewels are to be found on the sea-bed, look for the pearl-diver instead of running on the shore.'*" Fatima smiled as she handed him the book. "He's Ismaili, you know."

Fatima's voice seeped through Shamshu's body like a sweet nectar and rendered him speechless. She was suddenly so beautiful to him that he could barely look at her; he took the book from her and quickly turned his gaze down.

SOON AFTER THE DIAMOND JUBILEE was announced, a campaign was initiated within the jamat to raise the necessary funds for the diamonds. Council members visited businesses and requested donations. People gave what they could, grateful for the opportunity to pay homage to their Imam, who deserved their affection and gratitude for his great generosity and wisdom. Some people, like Mr. Jiwa, gave *karores,* thousands and thousands of shillings, and then in jamatkhana, when they read out his name and the amount he had donated (making many turn toward him with admiration and envy), Mr. Jiwa looked down and tried his best not to appear too pleased.

In an effort to emulate his father, a pillar in the community, Nizar decided to initiate a collection amongst the boys at school. Mr. Jiwa and Councillor Sahib were especially pleased when, after the list of initial donors was read, Nizar told them of the boys' collection.

Councillor Sahib tipped his head in the direction of Nizar and then said to Mr. Jiwa, "You've got a smart one there, *Bhai.*" He then shook his head in awe and patted Mr. Jiwa's shoulder with exaggerated effort.

"True indeed." Mr. Jiwa winked and then tossed Nizar's hair. There was no doubt in his mind whatsoever: he would make Nizar the sole heir to the business one day. God only knows, Shamshu would drive the company into the ground. "Hear that?" Mr. Jiwa asked Shamshu, who happened to be standing next to him. "See what a good example your brother is setting, hanh?"

Shamshu nodded, more out of habit than anything else. He was busy rolling a line of poetry in his mouth like a piece of candy. *Don't pretend to be a candle, be a moth.*

AT SCHOOL THE NEXT DAY, Nizar asked the boys to meet him outside, where he gathered them in a circle and announced his plans.

"Where do you think we're going to get the money, hanh?" asked Mussabhoy as he dipped his fingers into a greasy paper cone of chips.

Nizar snatched away Mussabhoy's chips. "Where the hell did you get the money for these, Fatso?"

"Eh, give them back!"

Latif shrugged. "Jiwa, he's got a good point, no? Where are we going to get the money?"

Shaking his head, Nizar turned to Latif. "Stay out of it, Latif. Who asked you anything?"

Mussabhoy reached up on his tiptoes, clamouring, once again, for his chips. "Give them back, otherwise I'll tell the prefect."

Nizar raised the paper cone higher above his head. "Tell the prefect, will you? Oh, and who do you think he'll believe, Fatso? A Jiwa or a tub of ghee, hanh?" He threw the cone down; chips scattered everywhere. "Come on, Fatso." Nizar waved Mussabhoy forward. "Want to make something of it?"

The other boys laughed and cheered Nizar on. "Jiwa! Jiwa! Jiwa!"

Shamshu stood at the outer edge of the circle as his brother pounded Mussabhoy. He turned his gaze up to the sky. It was so clear that it looked like a vast blue pool and in its reflection, Shamshu could see the Indian Ocean, filled with schools of fish and other creatures of the sea: whales, dolphins, seals, and mermaids. Suddenly, an idea occurred to him. He rushed to the boys, pushing them apart, and entered their circle.

"Pearls!" he said, loudly and clearly.

Nizar had Mussabhoy pinned to the ground, his fingers wrapped around his opponent's fleshy neck. "Have all the lunatics been let out today?" Nizar looked at the boys. "And to think we have the same mother, the same father."

Shamshu felt an unusual surge of confidence rise from his belly; he ignored Nizar. "Oyster Bay! That's the answer."

"What the hell are you talking about? Can't you bloody well see I'm in the middle of something?" Nizar kept his gaze fixed on his brother and gave Mussabhoy another slap. Mussabhoy wailed; Nizar cupped his hand over the boy's mouth.

"Oyster Bay!" Shamshu jumped up and down. "Don't you see? We don't need money. We can dive for pearls. We can give the Imam pearls."

Nizar climbed off Mussabhoy and walked to his brother. The other boys exchanged glances, some even raised their eyebrows. They liked Shamshu's idea, but no one dared interfere.

Nizar stared at his brother. "Well, well, well. What a bloody coincidence—exactly what I was thinking. Did you read my mind or something?" Nizar tapped Shamshu on the head, then winked at the other boys. "Plus we'll make it a competition. Whoever gets the most pearls will gift it to the Imam at the Diamond Jubilee. What a good idea, hanh?"

"Yes! A fine idea," several boys responded. They all clapped and chanted, "Hip-hip-hooray." They knew that despite his hot temper, Nizar loved a good and fair challenge and that victory was open to all. Most of them were avid divers. They would often dive for fistfuls of sand—with Nizar usually emerging the winner. But this time the stakes would be higher—not only would they have to find oysters with pearls (such fun!), but this would also provide them with a chance to do something for the Imam.

Shamshu did not mind that Nizar took credit for his idea. In fact he barely noticed that had happened. What bothered him was making the collection of pearls a competition. Why was that necessary? Why did it matter how much each person collected when it was all being done for the same purpose? To motivate people, to make sure they did their share? But wasn't the common goal enough? A goal that was greater than any individual accomplishment? Wasn't that the most important thing—what they all did together, rather than what they did individually? Besides, Shamshu had noticed, competition sometimes bred too much ambition, often putting things out of balance by singling out one person, who was crowned the winner, while the rest were thrown into one heap, all deemed losers. Not that it mattered, but Shamshu was certain he would never win—he was not built for athletics like Nizar. In fact, he usually only sat on the beach and watched the boys jump in and out of the water like flying fish. But it was the idea of finding a pearl, the search for a pearl, that shimmered in Shamshu's mind and spurred him on.

WORD ABOUT THE PEARL COMPETITION spread quickly throughout the school, generating a fever of excitement, so that practically all the boys signed up right away. Fatima wanted to sign up as well, but Nizar adamantly refused.

"Don't be ridiculous! It's for boys only."

"Are you scared that I'll beat you? I'm an excellent swimmer, you know."

Nizar and the boys laughed.

"I can see that's what you're worried about."

"Oh yes, I'm so scared." Nizar turned around, bent over, and pointed to his backside. "Look, I've even wet my pants!"

All the boys except Shamshu burst out in laughter. Fatima scowled at Nizar, then turned to leave, but he grabbed her arm. "Tell you what, girl. Why not be our timekeeper?"

Fatima tried to pull her arm away, but Nizar maintained his grip. "Plus, it would be a very nice bonus," Nizar winked, "to see you in your swimming costume. Come on, what do you say?"

Fatima pulled harder and as she broke free, her glasses slipped down her nose. "Idiot!" She scanned the circle of boys. "All of you—idiots!" She pushed her glasses back up with a finger and then wiggled her nose to adjust them into place. Fatima was about to leave when she noticed Shamshu, who was standing outside the circle. "Except you, Shamshu." She smiled at him. "How do you like Nasir-i Khusraw?"

Shamshu felt a surge of energy rise inside him like a wave, but it fell just as quickly when the boys began to tease him. You going to marry her, Shamshuji, are you?

Fatima marched over to Shamshu. "Don't listen to them! They're hooligans."

The boys continued their tirade. Think you can get it up for a girl like her? Maybe she's a real beauty under those Coke-bottle glasses, hanh?

Fatima took Shamshu by the elbow. "They're not like us," she whispered, and then led him away.

THE COMPETITION STARTED on the first day of the ten-day Diamond Jubilee celebration leading to the weighing ceremony. The plan was simple: spend the morning at the celebrations, which were held at the grounds of the Aga Khan Sports Club, the afternoon diving at Oyster Bay, and in the evening, return to the grounds for the special fireworks display that would, they were told, illuminate the sky in red and green, the colour of My Flag. The first morning, the boys wandered through the grounds with their families and visited various pavilions, which exhibited the work and activities of the community. Most of the boys concocted some sort of excuse and made it to Oyster Bay in time for the competition, but a few boys were disqualified even though they had valid excuses for turning up late; they had been forced by their parents to attend various lectures on topics like health and hygiene. They begged for leniency, but Nizar refused. "There is a price for everything," he told them, then waved them away.

The boys were provided with woven sacks made of *kikapu* and had thirty minutes to harvest as many oysters as possible. They all stood on the beach, one foot forward, anxiously waiting to start. The appointed timekeeper cupped his hands around his mouth. "On your marks. Get set. *Go!*"

The boys rushed into the blue-green waves and swam out several yards. Shamshu stood on the beach, watching as the boys gulped mouthfuls of air and then dove into the sea, their feet chopping the air before finally disappearing. They emerged a minute or so later, only to repeat the cycle. Go! Shamshu told himself. Don't be scared. He was unable to summon enough courage until he remembered a line from the poem Fatima had read to him: *Pearls and jewels are to be found on the seabed.*

Soon, Shamshu found himself stepping into the ocean and paddling his way to the boys. He repeated the line of poetry like an incantation, and when he submerged his head, his body shot downward like an arrow. Panic filled him. He thrashed his arms and legs violently until he was finally able to break his speed and descend at a slower, more manageable, rate. He then used his arms as rudders and came to a full stop, suspended in the water like a hummingbird in mid-flight. As he turned his head, he was overcome with the world he had entered. It seemed endless.

There was no sound except that of his own breathing. With each inhalation, his lungs filled with ocean water, and his heart, pumping to the rhythm of the waves passing far above him, distilled oxygen into his blood, and with each exhalation, it released a spray of bubbles and grains of salt through his nose. Shamshu felt as if he had merged with the ocean, filling him with a tremendous calm.

Moments later, a large, colourful fish with the curves of a woman swam by him. Shamshu was compelled to follow her. She led him downward, her tail swooshing through the water effortlessly. As they approached the seabed, Shamshu was forced to cup his eyes. A bright light shimmered from the mirrored floor. Shamshu swam closer to the bottom, drawn by its warmth. In the seabed, he could see his reflection clearly. He waved and made funny faces at himself. It made him laugh so hard that a continual column of bubbles escaped from his mouth, like an air pump in an aquarium. Soon, Shamshu propelled himself to a comfortable nook, sat down, and started to pluck oysters; he took his time and inspected each one with great care before placing it in his sack.

At the end of half an hour, the timekeeper called the boys back to shore, where they emptied their sacks of oysters onto the hot white sand and started to shuck them with great anticipation. Nizar had collected the most, about twenty, so he knew his chances of finding a pearl were better than anyone else's. He laughed out loud as he imagined all the praise he would receive when he gifted the Imam with the pearls. His father would be so proud!

Underwater, Shamshu suddenly felt a sharp, painful tug on his trunks, and before he knew what had happened, he was pulled up to the surface where Nizar and the other boys dragged him to the beach. Shamshu lay bewildered on the sand, his arms and legs splayed open, his hair sticking straight up, and at his side, his sack of oysters.

Nizar kneeled next to his brother, turned him to his side, and slapped his back over and over again. "I knew you shouldn't have gone down. Idiot!"

Shamshu couldn't speak. He continued to cough, not because he had water in his lungs but because his body was not used to being on land. The force of air being pushed down into his throat and lungs filled him with dread. He yearned to be back in the weightlessness of water.

The boys circled Nizar and Shamshu. Nizar straddled his brother. "Are you okay? Answer me, for God's sake." He shook Shamshu by his shoulders, then leaned down and placed his ear against his brother's heart—but it was beating so intensely that the sound pierced his inner ear and Nizar quickly retreated.

One of the boys reached down for Shamshu's sack of oysters, turned it upside down. Hundreds and hundreds of oysters fell out.

That night, Shamshu dreamt about Fatima. She was a perfume seller at bazaar and he, a nomad passing through her town. She sat cross-legged on a Persian carpet with tins of perfumes in the shape of fish sprawled at her feet. People walked by her stall, pinching their noses. Fatima spotted Shamshu in the crowd. She shot up from the ground and called out to him. "This way, my love. This way." Shamshu rushed to her like a wave to a shore and when he reached her, he fell to his knees, overwhelmed by her scent. As Fatima sat down, she took his head between her palms and led him down to her lap. She turned a bottle of perfume oil upside down onto her finger, then massaged it into his temples as she recited Pir Sadr al-Din's ginan "Sakhi Mari Atama Na Odhar" to him like a songstress. *"O Friend, the bed-swing sways back and forth with the rhythm of my every breath. O Friend, the saviour of my soul, do not go away and stay apart from me."*

BY THE NEXT DAY, word about Shamshu's success had spread through the celebrations like a firecracker over the sky. Nizar tried to downplay the stories, but they grew day by day so that they became impossible to stop. People longed to learn Shamshu's secret of staying underwater for so long. Some called him a master diver, others joked that perhaps he was part fish like Abdullah in *One Thousand and One Arabian Nights,* or that he had gills instead of lungs (after all, he had always been such an unusual boy); some speculated that he had cheated in some way (perhaps he had tied stones to his ankles like Gilgamesh), while the girls, even the prettiest ones, giggled and now stared at him with great admiration. Shamshu's father also congratulated him. "Finally showing your Jiwa side! Well done, son."

Shamshu was unaccustomed to all the attention he was receiving. He felt strange and awkward. He didn't quite understand why everyone was fawning over him. After all, he was only doing what came naturally to him, just as he had before, when he read poetry or spent the day imagining entire worlds. Why was this so different?

By day three, some of the men had organized daily bets on how many oysters Shamshu would harvest or how long he would stay under. Too much fun, *bana!* And because the community valued consistency and fairness, some men asked Shamshu to remove his trunks before each dive—so as to ensure that he was not using any sort of contraption. Shamshu obliged; he had nothing to hide.

Each day, growing crowds gathered to watch and cheer Shamshu on. Girls now arrived in groups with gifts of cake or handkerchiefs with their initials sewn next to his. One girl, the daughter of a shipping tycoon, even presented him with a twenty-four-karat gold bracelet. *Wa-wa!* yelled the crowd. But Shamshu refused the gift. "No thank you," he said. Shamshu had never fancied jewellery, especially the clunky gold rings and heavy chains that his father wore. The crowd shook their heads in disbelief. Don't be silly, Shamshu, you deserve it—you are a champion, *bana*. Go on now, you can't say no to such a pretty girl. Aye, other boys would kill for such affection! Several men grabbed Shamshu and held his arm to the shipping tycoon's daughter, her eyes sparkling. She smiled coyly as she wrapped the chain-link bracelet firmly around Shamshu's wrist. The men raised Shamshu's arm above him. The crowd clapped and hollered. Suddenly, a strange but infectious warmth swirled around Shamshu like an eddy and then pulled him into its centre, where he felt as if he was swimming, for the first time, with a school of fish instead of bobbing endlessly like a cork in the ocean.

When the men released Shamshu's arm, the sudden weight of the bracelet forced it down like an axe. His fingers tingled with numbness. Fatima, who had been standing outside the circle, broke through the crowd and handed Shamshu a note before rushing away. Shamshu could barely wrap his fingers around the paper. A sudden gust of wind blew the note out of Shamshu's hand. It fluttered away and landed at the water's edge. A wave swept in and carried it out to sea.

ON DAY SIX, Nizar, to everyone's surprise, dropped out of the competition. "What was the point of competing when there was no way of winning?" he had said to his father.

Mr. Jiwa reprimanded the boy. "Excuses will get you nowhere."

Nizar tried to protest, but his father refused to accept his arguments. Nizar felt cornered. If he competed, it would be in vain. If he didn't, he would be seen as a weak. For the first time, Nizar understood the perils of competition. How could it ever be fair if everyone did not have the same advantage? This thought suddenly made Nizar feel apathetic. It no longer mattered what he did. He mumbled some words to his father and then walked out of the house.

On the same day, Fatima was the first to spot Shamshu emerging from the water. She ran to him before the distant crowd swarmed closer. "Did you like the poem?" she asked, huffing and puffing.

Shamshu dragged his bulging *kikapu* sack out of the sea and onto the shore, his feet making deep imprints on the hot sand. "What poem?" he asked.

"The one I gave you yesterday."

"Oh yes, that one," Shamshu said. He did not want to tell her what had happened to her note, partly to spare her feelings and partly because he was more interested in emptying his sack and getting to the business of searching for pearls.

"So, did you like it?" Fatima asked as she tugged her earlobe.

"Yes, yes."

"My favourite part is the beginning. '*Stay close, my heart, to the one who knows your ways; not all eyes possess vision, not every sea ...*'"

The crowd, buzzing like a swarm of bees, clapping and waving their hands, approached from behind, drowning out Fatima's voice. They circled Shamshu like vultures. "How many today? How many today?" asked the men, many of whom had staked their week's earnings on today's bet.

Fatima continued, shouting over the men's voices. *"Not every sea is full of pearls. If ..."*

People stared at her in disbelief. Who did she think she was? Going on like that, speaking in tongues. Was she a lunatic, or what?

Shamshu surveyed the crowd and immediately realized that no one was interested in what Fatima had to say. He felt his face flush pink. He was embarrassed for her and wished for her own sake that she would stop. "Please, Fatima," he said, "why not wait until later?"

"But I was here first," Fatima retorted, and then continued her recitation.

Suddenly, Shamshu had the urge to put his hand over her mouth. "Shut up!" he yelled.

At first, everyone was silent, people looking at one another in shock, but then they erupted with laughter and thunderous applause.

Fatima stopped speaking, her eyes fixed on Shamshu.

Shamshu turned his gaze away.

"We have no use for you, girl," said one man, wagging his finger at Fatima.

"Exactly," piped in the shipping tycoon's daughter, a glint in her eye.

Soon, the crowd pushed Fatima out of the circle and tightened themselves around Shamshu like hands around a throat.

WITH EACH DAY, Shamshu continued to receive an abundance of praise from community members and leaders, not to mention the many gifts and notes of adoration from more and more girls. He had no idea that life could be this easy, this uncomplicated. A new question arose in Shamshu's mind. Why had he spent so many years spoiling his time with reading and writing when there was a more immediate path to love? It was those champions of the irrational—the poets! It was their fault. They had seduced him with the vague possibilities of union with the divine and the search for the meaning of life and truth. And what all for—fleeting moments of distilled joy? The external world, it seemed, was much more reliable. After all, it provided a defined path to follow and it provided so many rewards—instant rewards, not only with material value (because those are inconsequential really) but invaluable, intangible rewards like Respect and Recognition— things that had eluded Shamshu all these years. How could anyone blame him (or anyone else really) for choosing this path? It was natural, after all, to seek pleasure, not pain. And didn't a constant search inward create a life of loneliness, if not pain? Suddenly it all became clear to him: He had been putting his efforts in the wrong place. Shamshu vowed to carve out a path for himself, to make a name for himself in this world.

FOR THE TENTH and final day, the boys had agreed to dive in the morning so that they could all make it to the Diamond Jubilee weighing ceremony on time. Shamshu had forty-three pearls; the other boys had sixteen amongst them. Shamshu had clearly won, but even still, he was determined to collect more. He decided that he would aim for forty-nine—a multiple of seven to represent the seven heavens. In order to collect six more pearls, Shamshu knew he would have to start the final dive well before the other boys, especially since his typical daily harvest yielded only three or four pearls. Yes, he was bending the rules, but what of it when your goal was such a pious one?

That day, when Shamshu arrived at Oyster Bay, he found Fatima waiting for him. She presented him with a small paper cone filled with seven almonds. "To wish you luck," she said. "Open it." Inside, she had inserted a poem.

Because the meeting of two souls is never accidental. Yours, F.

> *From myself I am copper,*
> *through You I am gold.*
> *From myself I am a stone, but*
> *through You I am a gem!*

(p.s. I think Mowlana Rumi wrote this for Pir Shams.)

Shamshu scanned the page, barely reading it. "I have to go."

"It doesn't matter how many you find. It's the search that matters, don't you think? That's what will touch the Imam's heart."

For some reason, Fatima's voice now resonated with Shamshu, creating ripples through his body like a stone thrown in water.

Suddenly, he felt as though he was already underwater and that perhaps she was a mermaid, because his nostrils filled with the smell of fish. He leaned in, sniffed her neck.

Fatima stepped back. "What are you doing?"

Shamshu ignored her. An intense power surfaced from inside him. He continued to run his nose up and down her body. He started with the crown of her head, *sniff,* lifted her hair (oh, hair as smooth as pearls), *sniff,* her cheeks, *sniff,* opened her mouth with his fingers, *sniff,* nuzzled into her tender chest, *sniff.*

"Stop it!" Fatima said, her hands against his chest as she tried to push him away.

Shamshu fell to his knees and grabbed her foot, *sniff.* She fell backward onto the white sand; he climbed on top on her, *sniff.*

Fatima struggled but knew she shouldn't scream, because in the end no one would forgive a girl for coming to the beach unescorted. Instead, she pushed him with all her might and he toppled off her.

Fatima quickly stood up and dusted herself off. "Have you gone mad?"

Shamshu could hardly breathe. He rubbed his face in the sand and tried to shake off this overwhelming feeling.

Fatima was about to leave when she saw Shamshu's eyes through his sandy face—like an animal's in a cave—and she realized that he must be in love with her. Why else would he be acting like this? Yes, she knew it: they were soulmates. She had guessed this much the night of their discussion outside the library. After all, it was the first time she had met a boy who was almost as smart as she was. Fatima now wanted to know him as she knew herself— so that there would be no him, no her. They would be one.

"Please, will you take me diving with you?"

"Are you joking? My talent can't be shown. I was born with it." Shamshu stood up and turned back to make sure the other boys hadn't arrived yet. "Besides, I don't have time."

Fatima reached for him, letting her finger follow a trail of sand from his chin to his neck, circling the bulge of his Adam's apple, then continuing down his chest and stopping at the elastic waistband of his swim trunks.

Shamshu pulled her to him. "I can show. Come on, let's go."

Fatima pushed him back. "No." Why was he being so brash? "Not today—I have to go and get ready for the weighing ceremony."

Shamshu let her go, shrugging. "Fine. Your loss."

Fatima watched a wave crash to shore. "But I don't even have my swimming suit ..."

Shamshu leaned in and smiled. "It doesn't matter—come like that."

As they started their descent, Shamshu wrapped his hands around Fatima's waist. She squealed—a little nervous, but excited to discover his secret. Shamshu descended faster than she did; his hands slipped from her waist down to her knees. He looked up. He was keen to gauge her reaction—did she like it? Wasn't this wondrous? But her skirt had flown up and billowed out so that all he could see was the lower half of her body. She buoyed above him like a giant mushroom—her skirt, the cap; the pleats of her skirt, the gills; her legs, her strong legs, the stalk; and him, like Ganesha, the guardian to her watery femininity. He felt intoxicated under her and resolved never to let her go.

SHAMSHU ARRIVED at the Aga Khan Sports Club just before the weighing ceremony. It was hot afternoon and the grounds, which had the feel of a fancy country fair, were decorated with red and green flags and banners, strung with lights, welcoming the Imam. As Shamshu made his way through the crowd, looking for Councillor Sahib, he slipped his hand in and out of his suit jacket and fingered the little velvet bag that contained the pearls—forty-nine of his own (what an accomplishment!) and another nineteen from the boys. From a distance, it looked as if a faint tarnished light shone from under his body. Shamshu spotted Councillor Sahib, who, like the other dignitaries, was dressed in a long red robe and gold-coloured headdress.

Councillor Sahib took the velvet bag and shook Shamshu's hand heartily. "Well done, young man. You make us all proud."

Mr. and Mrs. Noorani, Fatima's parents, rushed up to them. "Councillor Sahib! Have you seen our daughter?" Mr. Noorani asked anxiously.

"Fatima?"

"Yes, yes. We are in a panic, Councillor Sahib."

Shamshu turned and inspected the grounds, which continued to fill with more people.

"Kamru-*bhai,* she's probably wandered off with her friends." Councillor Sahib stretched his arms out. "Look at the crowds here—over seventy thousand! The population of Dar has doubled because of the festivities, you know. Thousands have come from all over Africa—convoys of cars from Congo, Abyssinia, Uganda, South Africa, you name it. Not to mention all those who have come from India, the Middle East—even Europe, if you can believe."

"Yes, you're probably right. But as God is my witness, when we find her, she is going to get such a royal beating." Mr. Noorani shook Councillor Sahib's hand. "Thank you. If by any chance you see her, tell her we're looking for her." He then reached for Shamshu's elbow. "You too. Spread the word with your class-mates, *haya?*"

Shamshu nodded, shielding his eyes from the sun's glare, then turned to Councillor Sahib. "So you'll gift the pearls to the Imam during the ceremony?"

"I'll do my level best, young man. It's not in the plans, but let me see what I can do."

"Oh, I see." Mr. Noorani shook his head. "You are the fish-boy everyone is taking about, hanh? Such a brilliant boy! What is your full name, please?"

"Shamshudin Karmali Jiwa."

"Very good. You've made us all proud. Such a good example

for all the youth." Mr. Noorani cupped Shamshu's shoulder. "Please come for tea soon, okay?"

Shamshu nodded, and Mr. Noorani shook Shamshu's hand, then walked away with his wife.

The boys—with the exception of Nizar, who chose to sit with his sisters—found seats fairly close to the front. They were only twenty-some rows behind the first row, which was filled with merchant princes, representatives of the diplomatic corps, viziers to the Aga Khan and their Ladies, and the governors of Kenya, Tanganyika, and Uganda. People watched as title-holders from the Ismailia Volunteer Corps and other organizations paraded past in colourfully decorated floats. No one could wait for the Imam's arrival!

The precious diamonds, escorted by a fezzed Tanganyika police force, and contained in plastic bulletproof boxes, arrived at the entrance of the sports ground. People craned their necks and shook their heads in awe. But when the Imam entered, accompanied by his two sons and his wife, Her Highness the Begum, who wore a sari studded with fifteen hundred diamonds, people let out sighs and clapped. Many people wiped away their tears. They would cherish this moment forever. The Imam wore a robe of white and silver brocade studded with stars and a beautiful headpiece woven with gold thread. He waved at the crowd, then climbed to the stage, where He sat down majestically on a brocaded swivel chair. The chair was attached to a weigh scale the size of a small clock tower. Dignitaries sat on the stage floor just below Him. After a missionary recited a passage from the Koran, people who had donated the highest amounts were given a chance to place the first few boxes of diamonds on the scale. Slowly, the boxes of diamonds piled up. The Imam weighed in at over seventeen and a half stone, worth more than £640,000 in diamonds. The crowd stood in ovation.

Shamshu searched the rows of dignitaries for Councillor Sahib. He didn't want to miss the pearl-gifting ceremony, but he couldn't see the Councillor anywhere.

There were several other ceremonies before the Imam spoke. One presentation involved an eighteen-month-old boy, the son of a dignitary, who was brought to the stage and introduced to the gathering as a child of ideal health and physique. (Later, the boy was showcased in a special stall where his mother lectured crowds of other women on health issues.) Other presentations included ones by the Scouts and Guides, who bore banners from all the African territories, as well as individual gift presentations to Her Highness the Begum.

Finally, the Imam rose to the microphone. He thanked His spiritual children. "As everyone is well aware, the value of these diamonds has been unconditionally presented to me on this occasion. I do not wish to take this amount for myself but to use it for any object that I think is best for my spiritual children. After long reflection, I have come to the conclusion that the very best use I can make of it is that, after the expenses of these celebrations have been paid for, the whole of the residue must be given as an absolute gift to the Diamond Jubilee Investment Trust. This is not an ordinary investment trust such as you find in the City of London. While a considerable part of its capital must be used for investment in the ordinary sense of this term, a greater part goes to the building up of a totally new financial outlook among the Ismailis. Cooperative societies, corporations, and building societies will draw from the Investment Trust sums equal to their capital but at a level rate of three percent interest, and they are not allowed to charge more than six percent under any condition from their borrowers.

"Now one word, if I may be allowed to say it, of general advice to inhabitants here, whatever their race, colour, or creed. I have had some experience of the causes of strife and I was a very active member of the League of Nations and of the Disarmament Conference for some seven years. Why did it fail? Ultimately because of hate. And yet why did people hate each other? Fear. Where there is fear there is no love, but hate easily enters through the windows even if the door is shut. I appeal to all of you, Africans, Europeans, and Indians—do not fear each other. There should be none. Thanks to the atom bomb and the progress of knowledge and science, and if things take a turn for good instead of evil, then the new forces of nature, we are certain, will make human relations easier and give each and all security."

The community felt so fortunate, and many decided right then and there to name their future sons Diamond. The Imam's generosity and wisdom never ceased to amaze them. That day,

His Highness also conferred high titles like Vizier, Allijah, and Hazur Mukhi on deserving members. The Imam also married hundreds of couples, some whose families had made hasty wedding plans when they heard the Imam was coming.

After the ceremony, everybody lined up under the *mandap* and helped themselves to plates of *pilau* and *kachumber, dhar, ladoo,* and *ghatia,* and sipped on ice-cold sherbet. Shamshu and the boys chose not to eat; they were eager to find Councillor Sahib.

They found him trying to calm Mr. and Mrs. Noorani. "Listen, she must be here. You have searched everywhere?"

"Of course. We've looked and looked and can't find her." Mrs. Noorani clutched her handkerchief tighter between her hands. "Please, Councillor Sahib, please do something."

"*Bai,* I will definitely take up the matter after the ceremonies. Let's wait some. I suspect she's just lost in the crowd somewhere." He handed Mrs. Noorani a glass of sherbet. "Come now, have some. It will make you feel better."

Mrs. Noorani refused, saying she wasn't thirsty. "Something has happened to my Fatima," she said, wiping her nose with her handkerchief.

"No, no. Don't worry. I'm certain it's all just a misunderstanding of some sort."

The Nooranis left, still upset.

Latif turned to Councillor Sahib. "Tell us! Tell us. Were you able to give the pearls to the Imam?"

Councillor Sahib coughed, then looked away, waving at someone in the crowd before he reached into his pocket. "Of course. In fact, as with the diamonds, He has gifted these back to you." The Councillor handed the pearls to Shamshu. "Think you should be the one to keep these, no?"

Nizar watched from a distance as the boys clapped and cheered for his brother. "Shamshu! Shamshu! Shamshu!"

Shamshu took the bag of pearls, but his hand was unable to hold the weight and the bag slipped and fell to his feet. Several boys bent down immediately, and like servants in a king's court, they scrambled to pick it up for Shamshu. Latif prevailed. He placed the bag of pearls securely in Shamshu's hands.

Despite exhaustive search efforts, Fatima was never found. "If only ..." Mrs. Noorani would say to anyone who would still listen, "if only we knew the truth."

People tried to reassure her. "Probably the work of an African. You know how they are."

OVER THE YEARS, each time Shamshu heard this story, it calcified inside him, creating layers over layers like an oyster to a pearl, until he forgot the truth and believed the story himself. Shamshu never remembered Fatima struggling to break free of his grip—a grip that even he hadn't realized was so powerful; he didn't remember the bubbles escaping from her mouth, the terror in her eyes, and he certainly never felt her body go limp in his arms before slipping away and sinking down like a pirate's treasure. All Shamshu had been able to think about was his pearls, his precious pearls. And when he eventually surfaced, he became so engrossed with the task of counting the day's harvest that he forgot about Fatima completely. Although he did remember, and would repeat the story over and over again to his children and later his grandchildren, that he was a champion pearl-diver, capable of unheard-of feats. He was also able to recount the exact number of oysters he collected on each and every dive, and the praise, word for word, that had been showered on him (and still was).

By and by, Shamshudin Karmali Jiwa ended up a happy and successful man. Not only did he marry a beautiful woman and have three beautiful daughters and three ambitious sons, but he also ascended rapidly in the community and eventually became a Councillor himself; and despite Nizar's protests, Mr. Jiwa made Shamshu the primary heir to the family empire. The company was renamed S.K. Jiwa & Sons Inc., which although not intended, served as the final blow to Nizar, who left Dar es Salaam soon after and took a job as a porter at a shipping company in Dubai.

It was only on occasion that something niggled at Shamshu, like a fish bone caught in his throat, and he felt as if things were somehow off balance in his life, but then he would promptly conduct an inventory of all his accomplishments, which would, thankfully, remind him of who he truly was: S.K. Jiwa, business tycoon, community leader, family man. This put his mind at ease, for a while at least.

A Christmas Baby

As Layla Visram waited for the washing machine to complete its spin cycle, she rubbed her hand over her plump belly and wished she wasn't pregnant. She did not want another child. She was almost forty and her husband, Mansoor, was forty-three. They were, she felt, much too old. Besides, they already had three happy and healthy children: two daughters, Farzana and Sikin, aged fifteen and sixteen, and a boy, Ashif, who was ten. But more than anything else, Layla knew that they couldn't afford another child.

The economy in Alberta was in full recession and interest rates had skyrocketed to almost twenty percent. Local newspapers called it an oil bust and blamed the federal government for creating the National Energy Program—a policy that as usual, they said, unfairly favoured other provinces. In a matter of only months, oilrigs were shut down and construction companies abandoned their sites, leaving behind communities filled with skeletons of partially built structures—as if a monster-sized wrecking ball had swung through Alberta, smashing buildings and crushing thousands of people under its weight.

Visram's Speedy Gas & Convenience was one of the only stops on the lonely stretch of highway between Rocky Mountain House and Red Deer. Mansoor had purchased the business three years ago in 1979, and until last year, they had attracted a constant flow of customers—truckers delivering pipeline, oilmen on their way to a worksite, construction workers from nearby projects, tourists on their way to the Ice Fields Parkway, even motorists caught in a snowstorm. But nowadays, hours went by without a single customer, and for several months now, they had been unable to make their loan payments on time, prompting the banker, Mr. Snelgrove, to request a meeting.

The washing machine whirled to a stop and as Layla transferred her family's wet clothes into the dryer and set the dial to permanent press, she asked herself, as she had so many times before, Why didn't I have the abortion when I could have? Layla was now seven months pregnant; the baby was due on Christmas Day, which only added to her worries. Instead of being at school, the other children would be home.

MANSOOR PULLED open the interconnecting door that separated the store from their house in the back, and joined Layla at the kitchen table. The doctor's office had called earlier this week with the pregnancy test result. Mansoor was ecstatic about his new child. It was due on Christmas Day, can you believe? A Muslim child born on Christmas? *Wa!* What great blessings! Mansoor took this as a good sign—a sign of his family developing deeper roots in this new country of theirs. He turned to his wife and tried, once again, to reassure her.

"Please, you mustn't worry so much—especially now. It's not good for you or the baby. I'm telling you, Layla, we'll be just fine. There's nothing, absolutely nothing, to worry about." Mansoor craned his neck toward the living room to make sure that his children had not heard. The girls were sprawled out on the green shag carpet watching *Gilligan's Island.* Ashif was kneeling in front of the coffee table, his hand swooping through the air as he made a small plastic Superman fly around a building made of Lego bricks. Watching his son at play gave Mansoor tremendous joy and reminded him of his own childhood in Uganda.

Every Sunday, the entire family would pile into a caravan of cars made of Peugeots and a sleek new Ford, the trunks packed with huge *sufurias* of curried potatoes, sticks of spicy *mishkaki,* and *chapatis.* They sang and laughed the whole way to Lake Victoria. There the children would scatter, but always under the strict warning not to wander too far into the jungle or too close to the water. Once, when Mansoor was swinging on a tire roped to a tree, a crocodile emerged from the swampy lake and snapped its jaws at his heels. The other children ran away screaming but Mansoor pumped his legs faster and faster until he soared above the beast. Eventually, the crocodile tired and retreated back into the lake. When Mansoor returned to the other children, they clapped and cheered him on. The next day, he told and retold the story to all his friends, who shook their heads in awe as he boasted about his exceptional courage and prowess, and then pronounced himself The Master of Crocodiles.

Mansoor turned back to the kitchen table and anxiously reviewed a calendar on which he had mapped out his priorities, first for each week and then each day. At the top of each day's list, Mansoor would write an inspirational quote from one of his many business books, including his current favourite, *In Search of Excellence*. This week's quote said, *"What the mind can conceive and believe, it can achieve."* It was almost May month-end and he still had so many items under column A (Urgent): *Reconcile Accounts, Prepare Balance Sheet, Revise Cash Flow, Develop New Budget*. Mansoor was determined to make the loan payment on time this month. He adjusted the paper ribbon on his massive calculator, licked his index finger, and turned to the next page of the accounting ledger. He started by writing the auspicious numbers 7–8–6 on the top corner of the page—a practice his father had taught him in Kampala—and sure enough, he had always been able to balance the books to the exact penny.

Layla pulled her teacup toward herself, creating a line of wrinkles on the prairie wild roses of the tablecloth. "Please, just listen to me for once. I can't ..." She stopped and looked down into her filled teacup, the steam swirling at the rim. She knew he wouldn't listen to her reasons for wanting an abortion. But how in God's name could she take care of a baby in dire circumstances, yet again?

Only days before the expiration of General Idi Amin's November 8, 1972, deadline for all Asians to leave Uganda, Layla had arrived with the children at the Royal Air Force refugee camp sixty miles outside of London. Ashif was five months old, the girls, five and six years old. Months before, the Jewish community had been thrown out. Then the Asians, even the Muslims, were given ninety days to leave. Mansoor, like so many, had refused to believe the decree. "As if he'll throw us out! We were born in this country for God's sake." At jamatkhana, many leaders echoed his view. But then, as each day passed, more and more stories of Amin's terror began to emerge: two men murdered as they filled their cars at a petrol station; a man thrown into a car boot and never seen again; twin sisters, students at Makerere University, kidnapped from their dorm room and gang-raped for days by army officers before one sister finally escaped, her nipples still bleeding when she was found on the side of a road. Panic spread and the community started to pack their bags; the United Nations organized airlifts out of the country. They were allowed to take £50 with them, but Layla also managed to smuggle out some of her wedding jewellery by rolling necklaces into sweets like *ladoo* and concealing earrings in Ashif's milk bottle. The children's ayah, Rose, had cried as she handed the baby, wrapped tightly in the blue blanket she had knitted for him, back to Layla. "At least you have a way out," she had said, wiping her nose on the sleeve of her *kanga*. "What, Mamma, will the rest of us do?"

Layla had begged Mansoor to come with them—surely the British would show some compassion when they arrived in London. "Please, they will kill you," she said.

But Mansoor refused. He wanted to stay as long as possible, hoping like so many others that he might be able to salvage some of their fortune. Besides, he reminded her, the British Consulate had strongly advised against attempts to enter Britain without proper documentation. Illegal entrants, they warned, would be detained indefinitely, no matter if your wife and children were British subjects.

It is terrible, the consulate had said, this expulsion of eighty thousand Asians, but we have no choice: we must stand by our Voucher Quota System. City councils, like Leicester's, placed adverts in Ugandan newspapers like *The Argus,* urging Asians to stay away from their city. We have quite enough of them, thank you very much, quipped one councillor. Layla countered Mansoor's refusal by naming many other men who didn't have British passports but who were still going with their families.

"I'm not like other men," Mansoor said matter-of-factly. It was only when she started to cry that he took her in his arms and patted her back. "Be strong, darling, for the children's sake. Everything will be fine. We'll be together before you know it."

For many months, Layla had no idea where Mansoor was. Had he even been able to get out of Uganda? Why hadn't he listened to her? Yes, many of the illegal entrants were detained at the camps, but at least their families were together—and really, what else mattered? Layla would watch enviously as families clustered together at the camp cafeteria, eating and joking. Eventually, many of them even managed to emigrate successfully to countries like Sweden and Argentina, after spotting ads posted on the camp's bulletin board with the headline, HAVE YOU CONSIDERED EMIGRATING?

Mansoor's three sisters and their families had been on the same flight to London, but in the crowd at Heathrow, Layla lost track of them. She assumed they had been sent to another camp. Layla had two brothers, but both had settled in Kenya many years ago. She had even suggested to Mansoor that they could go to Nairobi. But by the time Mansoor agreed, all countries surrounding Uganda had sealed their borders. In London, Sikin and Farzana would constantly ask Layla when their father would be joining them. "Soon, bheta, soon," Layla would say as she tried to stretch her mouth into a smile. After a few months, the girls stopped asking.

The Uganda Resettlement Board urged everyone to get jobs quickly; London newspapers reported that many refugees were getting much too comfortable. Soon, representatives from various factories visited the camps and Layla was offered a job at a dress-making factory in Bolton, near Manchester; the job also included accommodations at a nearby boarding house. Before accepting the position, Layla tracked down Mansoor's sisters to ask for help; she was not yet willing to sell her wedding jewellery. Her sisters-in-law encouraged her to take the job. They said they would have gladly helped her, but their husbands were detainees and were therefore unable to work. Years later, Layla found out that their husbands had all successfully smuggled their fortunes out of Uganda. They had purchased tickets at Sabeena Airlines that went around and around the world, as if spooling the earth with miles of golden thread. Once they were in England, they quietly arranged for refunds.

In Bolton, the girls were sent to school and Sakar Bai Haji, an old lady from Kampala, took care of Ashif during the day. Sakar Bai had shared a room with Layla and the children at the camp in London and had begged Layla to take her to Bolton with her. "I know I am old, but look here—" She pushed up the sleeve of her maxi and flexed her bony arm. "You see? I am stronger than Shiva even. I promise, bheta, I won't burden you at all. Just don't you leave me here. I am all alone." Sakar Bai had stayed in Uganda for as long as she could, hoping to persuade her husband to leave. They will kill you, she said, begging him to join her. But he tied himself by the wrist to the door of his textile shop. "I was born in this country and I will die here only." There was already a sign on the window front: PROPERTY OF BARCLAYS BANK D.C.O.

That bastard Amin threw us out so he could snatch up all the property for the *golas,* but instead it was the British banks that ran away with all our money. *Arrey,* what kind of coup is that? Now I understand why they are always saying the sun never sets on the British Empire.

Each evening, Layla would return to the boarding house from the factory exhausted—not only from the physical labour but also from the constant effort required to understand what some of her co-workers and the floor manager were saying to her with their sharp English accents. She would make dinner on the hot plate in their room, then bathe the children and put them to bed. There were two single beds in the room. Sakar Bai took one, the girls the other, and Layla slept on some blankets on the floor with Ashif. Sometimes it was so cold at night, she worried that she would be unable to retain enough body heat to keep the baby warm. On those nights, she would warm her hands over the hot plate and press her hands all over his small body.

Months later, Layla received a letter, which told her that Mansoor was at an interim camp in Austria. Mansoor had sent the letter through a man at his camp who had relatives in London. The man's aunt had spent weeks making enquiries at all the camps before finding Layla in Bolton.

Layla and the children arrived at Vienna International Airport with a bulging brown suitcase and the winter coats given to them by the Women's Royal Voluntary Service. Layla spotted Mansoor immediately; he stood behind the glass wall of the crowded meeting area, holding his briefcase in front of him with both hands. He was wearing his wedding suit, a suit that he had special-ordered from London and would only wear at their anniversary dinner parties—parties that Layla would spend weeks planning, counting down the days as if it were their wedding day all over again. Hundreds of guests would come and the party would eventually spill into the back garden, but it always ended with Layla and Mansoor, alone, on their verandah at sunrise, sipping on a cocktail of sugarcane, coconut and passion fruit juice. They would sit across each other on the settee while Mansoor massaged Layla's feet, sore from wearing Marilyn Monroe–style pumps all night.

Only when Layla pulled the children closer to the meeting area did she realize how much weight Mansoor had lost. He used to look so dapper in that suit—complete with a white Oxford shirt, a red silk scarf tucked into the jacket pocket, and his metal-tipped leather shoes. Now, the dark blue suit hung on him like a gunny sack! Layla's heart sank, as if into a swamp, when she also saw that Mansoor had shaved off his moustache—a Marlon Brando moustache that she had convinced him to grow when they were first married. "You look just like Brando in my favourite film," she used to whisper, and then tiptoe to the other side of the bed, eager not to wake her in-laws. "You know the one. *The Ugly American.*" He'd chase her around the bed until he finally caught her. "Did I hear you correctly, Mrs. Visram?" "Yes, you did," she'd squeal, pretending to struggle in his arms until he picked her up and threw her gently onto the bed. "Well, it's true—anyone would be ugly next to you, darling, but please, I'm no American and I never will be."

When Mansoor raised his arms above his head, frantically waving at them, Layla's heart lifted as if it had surfaced for air, and she rushed toward her husband, Ashif bouncing in her arms and the girls trailing close behind. She felt like she had only enough energy to make it to his arms. But Mansoor reached first for his children, and Layla stood aside, watching as he twirled Sikin in his arms. "My God, Sikina-*sachu!* You're at least an inch taller." Then, he took Farzana's face in his palms. "*Wa-wa,* Falu! Look at you. Even prettier than Pappa remembers." But what brought tears streaming down his face was seeing his son, who was now over a year old, and walking. Mansoor tried to pick him up, but the boy screamed and locked his arms around his mother's knees. Mansoor pried his son away from Layla, despite his kicks and screams, and pressed Ashif tightly to his chest. He only returned the boy to Layla when people in the waiting area shot him dirty looks.

"Let's go, everyone," he said enthusiastically as he waved his daughters forward.

Mansoor never asked Layla how she had coped alone, and whenever she tried to ask him about his final days in Uganda or the camp in Austria, he just shook his head. "Oh-ho, Layla. What's the use in talking about the past?"

Now Layla wrapped both hands firmly around her teacup and gazed directly at Mansoor, who was expertly punching numbers into his calculator. "So, you tell me then," Layla said, her voice shaking. "How in God's name are we going to manage with another baby?"

Mansoor kept his head down. What the hell is wrong with this woman? he thought. Does she have such little faith in my abilities? Has she forgotten that I have always provided for this family—no matter what? Many at the Austrian refugee camp had seemed defeated, and succumbed to their new positions. At first, Mansoor also felt overwhelmed with everything they had lost. It was as if he had been on a giant wheel—one quick revolution and he was spun back in time. He was exactly where his father, Visram Govindji, a pauper from India, had been in 1912, at the age of thirteen, after surviving a wretched three-month journey on a dhow to arrive on the shores of Zanzibar with nothing but two rupees in his pocket and great hope for building a new life. Mansoor never imagined that his children might lead a life that was less fortunate than his. How could that be? Regression instead of progression. What kind of man, what kind of father would allow it? Not him! As each day passed at the Austrian refugee camp, Mansoor only deepened his resolve to charge ahead and rebuild their lives. They had been kings in Uganda and they would be kings yet again. He would do whatever it took to see that his children's lives were better than his, that they developed deep roots in whichever country they would now end up in (any country, but please, God, let it be a good country), so that they would never go through this again. Nothing else mattered. Yes, he would tell himself, each generation will grow stronger, not weaker, and one day, his progeny would herald him as a pioneer, just like his father in Uganda, who started one small dry goods shop in Tororo, on the Uganda–Kenya border, and then followed the new European railroad, eventually opening new shops at every stop: Busembatia, Iganga, Jinja, and finally, Kampala. "So you see," he would say to his children each Saturday morning when he marched them (and sometimes Layla) into his office and gave them a lesson on family history, "it can take a very long time to become good at something, but you mustn't ever give up. Hard work and determination! That is the only sure-fire formula for success. Everyone understand?" He would wait for a communal nodding of heads and then continue, "Mark my words—we will rebuild here in Canada, but instead of following the railway, we will just follow the oil patch."

Mansoor leaned over the kitchen table and erased an entry in his accounting ledger. "How many times can I tell you now, Layla?" He blew away the shavings. "Leave it to me. As if I haven't planned everything out, made all the necessary arrangements."

"But it isn't practical." Layla tried to control the tears pooling in her eyes. "Please, the doctors said we still have time."

"Aye-ya-ya, Layla. Leave it, I said! Can't you see?" He waved his HB pencil over the pile of neatly stacked manila folders. "I have so many bloody things to do."

Layla pushed her chair back with such strength that her teacup rattled on its saucer; she stood up and walked away, disappearing down the narrow staircase to the laundry room in the basement.

MANSOOR WAS NERVOUS as he welcomed Mr. Snelgrove, the Loans Officer from his branch of Alberta Imperial Bank of Commerce, into his store. Mr. Snelgrove was a tall plump man with a freckled face and bright orange hair buzzed to his scalp. The banker tucked his burgundy satchel, etched with the bank's logo, between his knees and then swept each arm with a gloved hand to remove the sprinkle of snow that had settled on his blue down-filled jacket.

"Not even Halloween and already got ourselves quite the dump of snow, eh?"

"Yes, yes. And minus twenty-eight with the wind chill." Mansoor reached for the banker's jacket; he was surprised to see that Mr. Snelgrove was not formally dressed. He wore a pair of black slacks and a pale blue shirt with a white T-shirt visible at the collar. Mansoor, on the other hand, was dressed in a dark grey suit, a crisp white shirt that Layla had freshly laundered and ironed, and a blue tie with red maple leaves. A terrible thought occurred to Mansoor: Was the banker trying, with this casual attitude, to ease him into some bad news? No! It's not possible. Wait until Snelgrove sees my new business plan—everything will be fine, Mansoor told himself. Think positively. He then took a deep breath and tried to slow his heart rate.

Mr. Snelgrove reached down to remove his galoshes, but Mansoor immediately stopped him. "No, no. Please, no need to worry about that." Mansoor knew that Canadians, like the British in Uganda, had the same filthy habit: they did not remove their shoes before entering homes. Earlier that day, Mansoor had laid a track of plastic from the interconnecting door to the entrance to his office, located next to the kitchen, and from the office to the bathroom, just in case.

"It's all right, Mansoor. They're quite a mess with all the snow and sleet."

Mansoor conceded and pulled open the door to the house. "This way, Mr. Snelgrove."

"It's been three years, Mansoor. Why don't you just call me Martin?" Mr. Snelgrove stepped into the house. "The bank doesn't believe in formalities. We take a fresh approach to things, you know."

Mansoor nodded. Three years, yes, but this was only the second time the man had taken the time to come to the gas station.

Inside, Mansoor asked Layla, who stood with her back to them washing dishes, to make two cups of coffee.

"Nice to see you again, Layla." Mr. Snelgrove raised a finger to the air as he followed Mansoor into his office. "And if you could make it two sugars, two creams, please."

Layla turned her head, her hands still in the sink. "Of course, Mr. Snelgrove, I remember," she said, smiling. She rushed to turn on the electric kettle. Please, God, let this meeting go well.

"Please take a seat, Mr. Snel... Martin," Mansoor said, motioning to the chair in front of his desk. Mansoor was about to sit down himself when he noticed Ashif's caged classroom gerbil in the back corner. Layla had refused to let Ashif bring home the rodent. He protested, saying that all his friends were being allowed to take turns signing out the class pet. Layla stood firm on her decision, saying she could understand having a dog for protection, like the Alsatians they kept in Kampala to guard the house, but she just couldn't understand the point of keeping such filthy animals—and to top it off, inside your house—for no reason at all except your own enjoyment. "Signing it out?" she had said. "What is it? A library book?" Mansoor hadn't liked the idea either, but when Ashif showed him the school newsletter, he changed his mind. Pets, it said, are an excellent way for children to learn about responsibility. Now, as the gerbil climbed into its exercise wheel and began to spin frantically, the wheel making a loud whirring sound, Mansoor was furious. Why had Layla put the cage in here? She knew that he was having an important meeting today! I swear that woman is going to be the end of me one day.

Mr. Snelgrove turned toward the cage. "Hey, what have we got here? Let me guess. Your new business plan calls for an addition of a pet store?" He smiled broadly and winked.

Mansoor laughed along as best as he could. "Oh, it's my son's, you see. Brought it home from school...." Mansoor stepped out from behind his desk. "Please, let me remove it."

"Oh no, let it be. We've got an Irish setter ourselves. My younger boy's hoping we'll get him a puppy for Christmas. Why not? It's a fine way to teach them responsibility. And it keeps them out of your hair too, eh?" Mr. Snelgrove let out a laugh that sounded liked a sputtering car engine.

"Exactly!" Mansoor knew he had made the right choice by letting Ashif bring home the animal. This was the Canadian way. Wait until he tells Layla what the banker said. Mansoor's spirits buoyed with confidence. He felt a strange kinship with the banker, and for some reason, he was now compelled to announce Layla's pregnancy. "My wife is expecting in December, you know? December 25th actually."

"Is that right? And a Christmas baby at that. Well, congratulations." Mr. Snelgrove leaned over the desk to shake Mansoor's hand. "You're going to have yourself a football team before you know it, eh?"

"Or maybe a hockey team." Mansoor laughed heartily as he placed a copy of the new business plan, like a menu, in front of the banker. He then stood behind his desk and started his presentation, waving his arms with great enthusiasm as he pointed to a series of colourful charts that were taped to the wall and contained phrases like BREAK-EVEN POINT, SALES VOLUME, and PROFIT MARGIN. The banker crossed his right foot over his left knee and removed a red felt-tip pen from his shirt pocket. As he listened to Mansoor, he lightly tapped the pen on the front cover of the business plan, making a constellation of red spots.

Layla came in, holding two cups of coffee and a plate of assorted cookies. Mr. Snelgrove congratulated her about the baby and then added, "Well, let's hope your Christmas baby gets Mansoor's business savvy and your looks, eh?"

Layla just smiled, but her mind travelled back to Kampala. She had been a bank teller at Barclays, where she had earned an excellent reputation over the years. She had even been promised a promotion to management, but then she learned that she was pregnant with Sikin. A few months after giving birth, she became pregnant again, this time with Farzana. Layla convinced Mansoor that she should return to work, but his father had adamantly refused. "What will other people say? That I am some sort of low-class fool sending my only daughter-in-law outside the house? Never. Not as long as I am alive. Besides, children need their mother." Her father-in-law died a few years later and Mansoor did not object when Layla returned to work at the bank. She was just re-establishing her reputation when she became pregnant with Ashif.

Layla placed the coffee mugs in front of each of the men; Mr. Snelgrove thanked her. The baby delivered a swift kick, but Layla held back any sign of pain. "Most welcome," she said, then returned to the kitchen.

As Mansoor approached the end of his presentation, he was sure he had impressed Mr. Snelgrove with all his research and figures. "As you can see, keeping the station open for 24 hours will increase sales by nine percent. Unheard of in this economy!

But I have all the figures to back me up. That's right. Nine percent, Mr. Snel... Martin."

Mr. Snelgrove slapped the business plan against his knee. "Well, it all looks pretty good, my friend, but my primary concern here, you see," he took a sip of his coffee, "is that your last four loan payments have been late." He reached into his satchel, removed a letter with a gold seal, and pushed it across Mansoor's desk.

Mansoor lowered himself into his chair and pulled himself to the desk. What was this? Was the bastard placing him in default of the loan? But he had paid each and every time, including the bloody seventeen-percent interest and the ridiculous late fees. Mansoor wanted to appear confident. He remembered his father's advice: *An elephant has two sets of teeth—one for eating and the other for showing.* As Mansoor picked up the letter, he tried not to pay attention to the gerbil, which continued to spin faster and faster in its wheel. He read the letter and then looked directly at the banker. "Yes, this sounds fine."

The banker seemed surprised by Mansoor's reaction. "Mansoor, you do realize that this is serious, don't you?"

"Yes, of course." As if he was an idiot. If only this stupid man could have seen me in Uganda. I've done more bloody business in one year than he will in his entire life. The letter meant nothing to Mansoor. It was, in his opinion, just another obstacle on the long road to success.

"If we were any other bank, we might've been putting you into receivership, but that's not at all how we like to operate. Your success is *our* success. I hate to be so formal, Mansoor," he cleared his throat, "but for legal reasons, I have to read the official warning to you." Mr. Snelgrove reached into his satchel and removed another copy of the letter. "'If Visram Speedy Gas & Convenience Incorporated (herein referred to as Visram Gas) is unable to remit loan payments on a timely basis for any reason whatsoever, then Alberta Imperial Bank of Commerce (herein referred to as The Bank) will place Visram Gas in default to The Bank, at which time The Bank will appoint the chartered accounting firm of Stanley Coleridge & Partners as receivers and the property and inventory of Visram Gas will be immediately liquidated.'"

Mansoor slipped his hands under his desk and cupped his knees. "I'm absolutely positive, Martin, no doubt about it. A hundred and fifty percent certain that keeping the station open 24 hours a day will turn things around."

"When is your sign arriving? The sooner you get it up, the sooner your business plan kicks in, eh?"

"Yes, of course. The installers were delayed. Some sort of a problem with staffing. A few of their men were sick. But I'm expecting them in the next few days."

"What's wrong with people these days? Used to be a time when a man could be dying and he'd still bust his balls to get to work. People today just don't seem to understand the value of hard work, eh?" Mr. Snelgrove shook his head. "They all need to be reminded that this great country wasn't built on men calling in sick."

Mansoor nodded enthusiastically. Once again, he felt a strong affinity with the banker. Snelgrove was right. A sick employee was hardly a good excuse for a delay. Was that any way to run a business? If they were my employees, I would have fired them on the spot. People should be bloody thankful to have a job in today's economy.

Mr. Snelgrove tucked the letter into his satchel and snapped it close. "All righty then, Mansoor. I think we're done here." Mr. Snelgrove stood up and then flung his satchel across his shoulder. "I'll give you a dingle a few days before your next payment, eh?"

"Yes, of course. Thank you very much." Mansoor's hand shot out to meet the banker's.

"No worries. That's what we're here for."

MANSOOR CROSSED OFF October 28th on the Alberta Imperial Bank of Commerce calendar, which was hanging on a nail hammered into the wall behind the cash register and had a picture of an oilrig silhouetted against an orange prairie sky. The 24-hour sign better arrive today or else, he thought, as he unzipped a grey canvas bank bag and emptied the money onto the glass counter. He arranged the bills into piles and stacked the coins into small towers before recording the amounts on a grid-lined sheet with the title *Daily Float*. After placing the money into the appropriate compartments of the cash register, he walked to the front window, which was covered with a light frost, and flipped the sign over to OPEN. Outside, snow swirled around the four gas pumps, the piles of sandbags, and a small freezer that was empty now but filled with bags of ice during the summer. Mansoor unlocked the double-bolted front door and unlatched the screen door. Layla had suggested that they also get an alarm system. "Anything can happen out here in the middle of nowhere." But Mansoor refused to raise his children under the impression that they weren't safe. As if this was the African jungle! Using his handkerchief, which was inscribed with the letter *M,* Mansoor tried to wipe away the frost on the window, but instead, he created a pattern of semicircles, like smudgy rainbows all over the glass.

Mansoor tucked his hands into his pockets and surveyed his store as he did every morning. The wall to his right was covered with a mural of Hawaii—a towering palm tree, an endless white sand beach, and a blue-green ocean. He had papered it himself, hoping it would brighten the place up. And it certainly did! It always reminded him of Kampala (even if Kampala was more beautiful) and most especially, it reminded him of the family picnics at Lake Victoria. Today as he looked at it, it also made him think about his Christmas baby and he was filled with tremendous hope. The new baby, thank God, would not be tainted by history. Born here. Not there. It will give us a fresh start in this great new country of ours.

It was a small store, Mansoor thought, as he continued his inspection. Only 522 square feet but—he smiled proudly to himself—it was very clean and expertly merchandised. When they had first purchased the gas station, there was only a payment booth. But within a year, Mansoor expanded and built the store. He conducted surveys of all his customers and consulted with the local Chamber of Commerce on traffic patterns and other vital data in order to develop the right selection of products to carry. The store had four aisles: Fishing, Camping, Sundries, and Snacks. High-profit items, like chocolates and fish bait, were shelved at eye level, while lower-profit items like kerosene oil were on the bottom shelves. In the back were two coolers filled with soft drinks—although many of the slots were empty these days; they hadn't reordered as they were worried about carrying too much inventory. Next to the pop coolers, on a dark-brown Formica counter, was a Slurpie machine fitted with two nozzles (Coca-Cola and root beer were the number one sellers in winter, Coca-Cola and cream soda in the summer) and a self-serve coffee station with packets of sugar, NutraSweet, and Carnation Instant Milk Powder, each stuffed into separate Styrofoam cups. Behind the cash register were glass shelves partially stocked with cigarettes. Under the shelves was a blue milk carton with a small collection of used books including Danielle Steel's *Promise,* The Hardy Boys' *The House on the Cliff,* and Arthur Miller's *Death of a Salesman*—books that were traded in or purchased by summertime campers. In a locked drawer, they also kept a few adult magazines. A clear sign warned: YOU MUST BE EIGHTEEN OR OLDER TO PURCHASE CIGARETTES OR ADULT MAGAZINES. Layla had suggested the idea after noticing the many semi-trucks that had cartoons of naked women on their mud flaps. Mansoor was surprised by her suggestion (leave it to her to notice such *poozee* details), but he had agreed because it would be yet another way to increase sales. Layla was a practical woman, Mansoor thought, but sometimes a bit too practical. (How in the world had she even been able to suggest an abortion? There are times, he told himself, when a man must not compromise.)

He reviewed the shelf signs in each of the aisles. Special promotions were highlighted with signs stencilled, under his close supervision, by Sikin and Farzana. He had developed an efficient process for the weekly production of new signs and was proud that he was teaching his daughters the value of hard work. He would come up with the promotional idea, then write the copy in a book chained to the front counter—*Buy 2 Get 1 Free ... Speedy Gas SuperSaver.* The girls were given several markers to choose from (red, black, or blue) and two days to complete the work, after which they received one dollar for each sign they produced—not counting, of course, the ones that were not approved due to errors (and therefore thrown away) or the ones that did not meet his deadline.

Layla pushed open the interconnecting door, holding two brown paper bags and a green Incredible Hulk lunch kit. She yelled into the house, "*Jaldi-jaldi!* The bus is going to leave."

The children rushed past her, grabbing their lunches on their way to the front door. Sikin rooted through her lunch bag, removed a Saran-wrapped sandwich and waved it above her head like a flag. "Cheese and tomato again?"

"It's good for you," Layla said as she shuffled behind the children in her thong slippers and terry-cloth robe, under which she wore a threadbare yellow nightgown made of *kanga* material patterned with red giraffes and green acacia trees. "Get a proper nightgown, will you?" Mansoor would scold whenever she wore the *kanga*. "You'll catch a bloody cold in that thing. This isn't Kampala." Layla loosened the robe's belt, which was tied under her breasts—breasts that were now, to her dismay, double their original B cup. This pregnancy had been nothing like the others. She had retained so much more water; her fingers were fat sausages, making simple tasks like washing dishes or doing the laundry difficult, and her feet were balloons, making walking painful at times. She had also put on more weight than before, an extra thirty pounds. It was as if the baby, like a cancerous lump, was swelling inside of her at an exponential rate and pushing her to the outer edges of her own body. Soon, she felt, she would fall out of herself completely.

Layla walked toward Sikin, one heavy step after the other. "But this time I used Velveeta, bheta. Just like you wanted. It will taste so nice, you wait and see."

"Yeah, fine," Sikin mumbled, and pushed open the screen door.

Mansoor shook his head as he watched his children. They were late again! Why couldn't Layla organize them more effectively? She knew full well that the bus arrived at 8:21 on the nose, each and every morning. Rushing around like this was no good for them. Had they even eaten their breakfast?

The girls waved goodbye as they stepped out into the cold. Layla pulled Ashif's Edmonton Oilers toque over his ears and kissed him through the orange scarf wrapped around his neck and face. "Learn lots today, *mitu.*" Ashif nodded, then hurried behind his sisters. A drift of snow blew in, covering the floor and Layla's feet. She unknotted the belt around her robe, then cinched it more tightly across her body as she watched the children run toward the service road, leaving a track of fresh footprints in the snow. The girls stepped onto the Rocky Mountain County school bus and disappeared among the other children who were from nearby farms, acreages, and trailer parks. Ashif turtled behind his sisters in his thick snowsuit. When he finally reached the bus and tried to climb in, he missed the first step, falling flat on his bottom. Oh no! Layla automatically reached for the door handle, but as she pushed open the screen door, her feet slipped on the slick floor and she lost her balance.

Mansoor's voice shot through the aisles like a bullet. "Careful!" he yelled, and rushed to her.

Layla had caught herself in time. "I'm fine, I'm fine." As she steadied herself between the door frame with both hands, a thought occurred to her: What would have happened if I had fallen? But she quickly shook the idea out of her mind.

Outside, Ashif struggled to get up; his knapsack seemed to be weighing him down.

"You mustn't spoil him," Mansoor warned. "As if he's a baby."

Ashif pushed himself up from the ground and dusted the snow off his pants.

"See that?" Mansoor pointed to his son, who was now climbing onto the bus. "He's fine. Bloody well going to make the children so *phocha-phocha* that they'll just fold over with even the slightest difficulty in life. Is that what you want? Is that how we made kings of ourselves in Uganda?"

Layla pulled the screen door shut. She was just glad that Ashif was wearing thick snow pants.

Mansoor continued. "I'm asking you, Layla, is that what you want?"

Layla turned around, marched straight past him, and disappeared back into the house.

LAYLA WAS STANDING on a small stepladder, busy dusting the cigarette shelves with a J Cloth, when a delivery truck pulled into the gas station. The truck was plastered with bumper stickers, one which read, LET THE EASTERN BASTARDS FREEZE IN THE DARK. The front door jingled. She steadied herself on the counter and carefully stepped down. She was happy to see a customer: a large burly man with a sheepskin hat and a down-filled jacket with the name Stu embossed on an oval patch. Stu stamped the snow off his boots and nodded hello as he walked to the counter and then slid a clipboard of papers to Layla. A pen attached to a worn-out string rolled out.

"All I need is your John Hancock, ma'am. Top copy's going to be yours."

Layla examined the form. Across the top it read: ROCKY MOUNTAIN SIGN COMPANY. At the bottom it was stamped with the words: Balance due in 30 days. "What is this?" she asked.

The man pointed outside to his truck, the roof covered with mounds of snow. "The sign you ordered, ma'am. Rush delivery as requested."

Layla checked the order book chained to the back counter, in which Mansoor diligently tracked all orders, delivery dates, and outstanding invoices. The pages were bare. "But we're not expecting anything. Are you sure?"

"Yes'um, I sure am. Says Visram's Speedy Gas right here," he said, tapping the invoice. "Can't imagine there's another one with that name for many miles around, eh?" He grinned and leaned an elbow on the glass counter.

Why had Mansoor ordered a sign instead of asking the girls to make one? "One minute, please. Let me get my husband."

Layla returned with Mansoor, who signed the papers right away. "Finally," he said as he ripped off the top copy.

"Sorry about the delay. Couple of the boys were down with that nasty flu that's been going around. But we'll get you set up nice and good. We appreciate your business, no doubt about it." Stu slipped the clipboard under his armpit. "How's business with you folks?"

"A little slow right now." Mansoor folded the invoice in half and creased it with his thumbnail. "But I'm sure things will pick up soon."

"I sure hope so. I'm telling you, if it wasn't for them bloody feds—goddamn Trudeau—we wouldn't be in this situation."

"Yes, it's terrible really," Mansoor said, even though he was a bit put off that this man was blaming Trudeau. After all, if it wasn't for Trudeau, God only knows what would have happened to them. At Uganda's independence, the British had promised to protect all those who were worried about a fever of excessive African nationalism and therefore wanted to maintain their passports. But without Ugandan citizenship, the new African government would not allow Asians to operate their businesses. So what to do? Stay in the safe middle, what else? Let your wife maintain a British passport and you get a Ugandan passport. Such bloody irony, Mansoor thought. Amin threw us out because Asians had split loyalties. Why hadn't you chosen to become Ugandan citizens at the most critical time in the country's history? You have milked the cow, but did not feed it. Some said that Amin threw them out because an Asian family had refused his request for their daughter's hand in marriage. (But who, in God's name, would let their daughter marry an African even if he was the president?) And then, the Queen denied entry for those without passports even if they were stranded in Uganda and their families had been airlifted to London. *Stuck* in the middle, more like it.

After the expulsion order, Mansoor had made many attempts to secure proper British documentation. Each night, many men, their sons in tow, camped outside the British High Commission to secure a good position in the long lineup. The Commission could only process so many refugee applications each day, yet they refused to extend their limited hours (10 A.M. to 12:30 P.M. and 2 P.M. to 4:30 P.M.). During one of the lineups, a man whose application had been denied quipped, "When the British came to Uganda, they didn't need passports. Why do we need them to go to Britain?" Many countries, like America, had turned their backs. But not Canada. Pierre Elliott Trudeau generously opened Canada's borders to Uganda's Asians, including the Ismailis. The Aga Khan and Trudeau had been longtime friends, both of them Harvard alumni. Trudeau, if you can believe, even made time for the negotiations during the final game of the nail-biting Soviet–Canada hockey series! The Imam assured Trudeau that Ismailis would be self-sufficient. They were, after all, self-starters, entrepreneurs, civic-minded people who would add to Trudeau's vision of a multicultural Canada. (During one of their history lessons, Mansoor told the children that the Prime Minister had rescued him by pirouetting into the Vienna Refugee Camp in a red cape and beret with a maple leaf on it, before scooping him up and away like a superhero. *Merci beaucoup,* Monsieur Trudeau. *Merci beaucoup.*) Since their arrival ten years ago, Mansoor had insisted on keeping a small framed picture of the Prime Minister next to the larger one of the Imam. He also insisted that he and Layla vote Liberal; Layla agreed (he hoped) even though she said there was no point in voting, especially during provincial elections. What difference could they make? There had been no change to Alberta's Conservative government for decades. "That's not the point," Mansoor retorted. As usual, she didn't understand even the simplest of ideas.

"We got to get that Trudeau out," Stu continued. "'Member all the good years—before all this National Energy bullshit? Jumping Jesus! The construction crane was the provincial bird and all a man had to do to earn a living was get out of bed." Stu scratched his neck and then pointed to the shelf behind Mansoor. "Give me a pack of Player's, will ya?"

How could Mansoor forget those years? If only he had been in a position to take advantage of Alberta's booming economy. But he had spent the first seven years working double shifts at a dry-cleaning plant in Calgary and shovelling sidewalks in order to save enough money to make the required down payment on some sort of business. Business—that was the only way, the *only way* to own land, to call something your own. He wished he had more family here; that way they could have invested in a business together. But all three of Mansoor's sisters had settled in the U.K.—although, with Thatcher in power now, jobs were no longer stable and many were keen on immigrating to Canada. Mansoor hadn't said anything to Layla yet, but he had started to investigate how he could sponsor their families to come here. It was, after all, his duty as their brother to help them out.

When they first arrived in Canada, Layla had suggested that she could work too; she reminded him of her experience in banking and pointed out that she now had Western work experience by way of the dressmaking factory. "You're going to kill yourself working like this," she said. But Mansoor refused. Ashif was only a baby and the girls were so young. His father was right: children need their mother. Especially in this country with no family around. Besides, Mansoor had no doubt that he could do it himself. Things will get easier, he would tell himself as he applied various chemicals onto the suits of other men. This is not for the rest of my life. No! He wasn't like the other workers at the plant who had never tasted another kind of life, who easily accepted their mediocre lives. This was as good as it got for people like them. He had been so thankful that Immigration Canada had sent them to business-minded Alberta.

"Soon enough things will change, you know," Mansoor said as he handed Stu a pack of cigarettes. "Business is like that. All about cycles."

"I suppose so." Stu tore the cellophane wrapping from the packet of cigarettes, and crumpled it before placing it on the counter, where it crackled open. "But the way things is going these days, I don't know. It's enough to make a good man a thief, eh?" He laughed, sliding open the pack of cigarettes and offering one to Mansoor.

"No, no. I quit many years ago," Mansoor said proudly.

"Well, if I had a pretty wife like yours, then I woulda quit for her too."

Layla blushed as she reached for the cellophane wrapper and then tossed it into the garbage. She was the one who had made Mansoor stop the first time, soon after they were married, but he restarted the habit when they first moved to Canada. For years, Layla had begged him to quit, but he only did after Ashif told him about a competition at school. Whoever could get their parents to quit smoking would receive a pair of hockey tickets to see the Red Deer Rustlers.

"But a man's gotta have some sort of vice if he's gonna survive, eh?" he said, winking at Mansoor. "Well, I best set the sign up for you." He raised his arm to them and then turned to leave. "Good luck to you all."

Layla followed Mansoor back to his office, her worn-out penny loafers squeezing her swollen feet. "What kind of sign costs this much money?" she asked.

Mansoor didn't say anything. How many times did he have to tell her to leave the business to him? Stop interfering! He reached into a brown accordion file, pulled out a piece of paper, and slapped it on his desk. "Look at this. Red neon," Mansoor said, hardly able to hold back his excitement. "It'll get people's attention—especially at night." The paper had several lines and measurements under a sketch of block-shaped letters with the words OPEN 24 HOURS.

"Twenty-four hours?"

"Exactly! If we can tap into the traffic at night, it will definitely boost business. Look here." Mansoor picked up a red felt pen and pointed to the same colourful charts he had showcased to Mr. Snelgrove. "The X axis represents nighttime traffic numbers, categorized by vehicle type, semis, passenger ..." He continued, explaining his new business plan, which included offering specialty coffees and fresh doughnuts. "You wait and see, even the cop-*las* will become regular customers." Another point: aggressively market the fact that people can park overnight in the abandoned lot next door. There weren't any motels for miles, and what do those poor truckers do if they are sleepy or, worse yet, if they're caught in a snowstorm? In the same way that they had expanded by adding the front store, this would be another phase of growth for Visram Speedy Gas & Convenience. Maybe phase three would include a bar and restaurant with large televisions where locals could watch the number one pastime, hockey. Mansoor didn't expect Layla to understand the details of the plan, but suddenly he felt very pleased with himself. This wasn't just a matter of surviving the recession: this was another step in growing the business. Yes! It was going to be a good year. He would turn the business around, and with the Christmas baby arriving soon, this would be the beginning of their new life here, the kind of life they were supposed to be living.

Memories of Uganda swelled in Layla's head. "But anything could happen at night …"

Mansoor clucked his tongue. "Could you listen for even one bloody second?" He went on to explain that a doorbell would be installed and nighttime customers would ring for service. This way the store would be locked most of the night.

"Please, I don't want you to work at night. It's too much. You're going to kill yourself working like this."

Madre-chod! As if he couldn't bloody well manage it, Mansoor thought. Hadn't he survived much worse? He was fully capable of managing a 24-hour business. He was in excellent health. Did he have to remind her that he had been the boxing champion in the Lightweight Asian Division? Didn't they even liken him to Muhammed Ali? Hadn't people joked during the Ali–Foreman "Rumble in the Jungle" match that Mansoor should drive to the Congo and replace Ali? Why couldn't she see him for who he really was?

"I'll rest in the afternoon, and until the baby comes, you can work part of the day. Plus the girls are now old enough to start taking a little bit more responsibility. They will work at the front counter for a few hours after school and on the weekends." Mansoor pulled out a calendar on which he had already worked out their schedules.

A sharp pain shot up Layla's legs and into her back. She folded her arms over her belly. What kind of life was this for the family? This was no condition to bring another child into the world. Bad enough the children never got a chance to go anywhere. Always stuck here, in the middle of nowhere. And now there would be bells ringing all night? And what about going to jamatkhana? There was a small community in Red Deer that congregated for prayers in a hall. The family had been able to attend Friday ceremonies once in a while, and more important occasions like Kushali or Chandraat, but now they would never be able to get away from the business. And what about the Imam's Silver Jubilee Padrami next year? All other families would surely be going to the celebrations, even taking many days off to go to Edmonton or Calgary, Vancouver and Toronto just so that they could all be together for *deedar*. For that matter, some would even charter planes from the world over, just as they had during the Imam's first Canadian visit in 1978. Bad enough the children don't get a chance to socialize with other children from the community, but not attending Padrami? This is worse than the jungle! Layla knew she wouldn't be able to convince Mansoor, so she offered a compromise. "At least have an alarm system installed?"

"Eh-ma, Layla. You have become a radio-*mbafu*. Same story all the time." Mansoor tapped his pen like a drumstick on his palm. "Listen carefully this time. This isn't Uganda. We've been here for ten years now. For God's sake, when will you bury Uganda in Uganda?"

The front door jingled and the children came roaring into the house. Layla turned and rushed to the kitchen. She still had to make dinner.

In late november, the girls had asked their father if they could decorate the store with Christmas ornaments and maybe even get a tree. "Of course!" Mansoor was so proud of his daughters. They had easily taken on the responsibility of working at the store, and on top of it all, they were showing great potential by initiating new ideas like this one.

Now Layla was perched on a stool behind the counter, her arms crossed over her swollen belly, as she watched her daughters.

"Mummy, can we buy Christmas presents?" Sikin asked as she held a stencil of the nativity scene against the front window. Farzana vigorously shook a can of artificial snow and sprayed in Baby Jesus.

"Isn't your new baby brother or sister enough of a present?" Layla said, even though she had already bought each of them a small gift: a Judy Blume book, *Deenie,* for Sikin; a box set of nail polish for Farzana; and a Marvel comic, *Captain America versus The Incredible Hulk,* for Ashif. She had decided to give them the presents on December 13th, the Imam's birthday, especially since they would not make it to jamatkhana for the celebrations.

"As if a baby could ever replace anything." Sikin delicately wiped away an error on Joseph's face, her finger wrapped in a Viva paper towel.

"I hope it's not a boy. Who wants another brother?" Farzana overfilled the Virgin Mary by mistake; a glob of snow oozed down her body, leaving an empty strip in the middle of her.

Just then, Mansoor walked in from the house, his arms filled with boxes of Christmas lights purchased at Canadian Tire. "It doesn't matter if it's a boy or a girl, as long as it's healthy." He placed the boxes onto the counter.

"Exactly, as long it's healthy," Layla echoed as a sharp pain shot up her legs and into her back.

"Look, girls, I have lights. Red and green." Mansoor waved a box above his head. "We can string them over the Hawaiian palm tree and it will feel just like Kushali in Kampala, huh?"

The girls nodded enthusiastically. "Great idea, Pappa."

Layla shifted on the stool, trying to find a comfortable position, while Mansoor opened the box of chocolates sent by Mr. Snelgrove. The attached card had a picture of the bank's employees in front of a towering Christmas tree. Inside, in red script, it read, *All the best this holiday season. From our family to yours,* followed by many signatures, none of which Mansoor recognized. He also didn't recognize anyone in the picture except Snelgrove, who had written in above his name, *We appreciate your business.* Mansoor felt great satisfaction in these words. He had made the last bank payment on time—a day early in fact—and Snelgrove had obviously made note of it. Mansoor knew how bankers, like all good businessmen, operated. Gifts never arrived without some hidden meaning: Snelgrove was obviously trying to butter him up, certain that Mansoor would one day be a business tycoon. Mansoor held the card open like a wishbone in front of Layla and pointed to the banker's message. "See. Didn't I tell you everything would be fine?"

Layla didn't bother reading the text. Her mind was occupied with all the preparations required for the baby's arrival. "*Inshallah,* business will improve." She leaned forward and reached into the box of chocolates.

"Will improve? Already sales are up significantly." Mansoor tapped her hand away. "*Arrey,* don't just take any one. Check first.

Don't you know that many are filled with all sorts of rubbish—rum, Irish cream, and who knows what else?" He examined the descriptions on the inner lid of the box and chose one, the shape of a finger, and handed it to her.

Layla shook her head.

"Who's saying don't have one?"

"Bas," she said, focusing her gaze on the girls. "I don't want one. I lost my craving."

Mansoor laughed in surprise and frustration. But it's for her own bloody well-being! I'm telling you, there's just no satisfying this woman. Even when things are starting to look brighter, she still insists on spoiling everything. If only this woman supported me rather than always causing problems, then surely, we would fulfill our dreams much quicker in this new land. I don't know when she'll learn to be more co-operative!

IT DIDN'T TAKE Mansoor long to become accustomed to waking up to serve customers. On some nights, especially the weekends, the traffic was quite heavy, interrupting his sleep seven or eight times. Yes, he was a little tired, but it was all worth it, he would tell himself. Besides, it was crucial to take advantage of what he called "Christmas traffic"—people returning from parties or on their way to visit family. Also, night customers were willing to pay more and surely they would start turning a profit soon. "Might as well get used to waking up, Layla," he would say if she suggested that he turn off the 24-hour sign so that the family could have at least one peaceful night. "The baby is due soon."

Layla pulled the bedcover over the mound of her belly and tucked it under her chin. Her lower back was throbbing with pain even though she had taken an aspirin earlier that night. She preferred not to take any medication during the pregnancy, but tonight, she could not bare the pain. She hadn't told Mansoor, certain that it would spoil his sleep; he would be up all night, worried about whether the baby was all right.

"You've become such a *toon-toon*," Mansoor teased, tapping Layla's belly.

"It's going to be a big baby," Layla said.

"Of course. A Canadian baby. What do you expect? Maybe even a hockey player, huh? Who knows, you might be carrying the next Gretzky in there." Mansoor laughed as he folded his *Red Deer Gazette* in half and tossed it onto the shag carpet. Layla rolled over to her side and pretended she hadn't heard him.

Mansoor had just switched off his bedside lamp when the front bell rang. "Customer," he said, and quickly slipped out of bed. He grabbed his suit jacket from behind the bedroom door and put it on over his pyjamas as he rushed down the long hallway.

A black Bronco truck with red and orange flames covering its front cab was parked in front of gas pump number three. Mansoor flicked on the pump switch, and then buttoned his suit jacket, tucking his pyjama sleeves up and out of sight. Outside, a short muscular man wearing a Santa Claus hat removed the gas nozzle. Next to his truck with its raised monster-sized tires, the man looked like one of Ashif's action-figure toys. Mansoor chuckled out loud at his comparison. Yes, a tiny Incredible Hulk. If only he was green!

The Hulk replaced the nozzle and ambled over to the truck, where he rapped his knuckles against the tinted window and cocked his head toward the store. A lanky man with long, straight blond hair jumped out. A mangy German shepherd followed. The Santa hat slipped down the Hulk's forehead as they headed toward the store. Mansoor rushed to unlock the front door; he stood aside and held the screen door open with an outstretched arm. His customers came in, the dog following, sniffing at Mansoor's feet.

"Sorry. No dogs in the store."

The Hulk hiccupped as he pushed up his Santa Claus hat to reveal his glassy green eyes. "I know, for fuck's sake. Rocco here is just taking a piss. You heard the man, Rocco. Git!" The dog shifted from one front leg to the other and then took a cautious step forward. The Hulk jabbed his cowboy boot into the dog's belly. "I said git!" The dog darted out, yelping.

Mansoor closed the front door and followed the customers to the cash register, where the Hulk threw a few bags of Cheezies and a Mars bar on the counter.

"Is that everything, fellows?" Mansoor asked as he rang in the items.

The Hulk leaned into the counter. "How's about a package of Export A's? Oh, and looky here, Scotty." The Hulk pointed to the sign: YOU MUST BE EIGHTEEN OR OLDER TO PURCHASE CIGARETTES OR ADULT MAGAZINES. "What do you think, Scotty?" He turned to his friend, who stared blankly, his hands shoved deep into his jeans pockets. "Come on now, Scotty, don't be shy. The man ain't going to bite you or nothing." He yanked Scotty's arm and pulled him closer to the counter. "Come on. I know you want some. Just tell the man."

Scotty's cheeks flushed red. "Can I please have a *Hustler*?"

"Atta boy, Scotty!" The Hulk slapped his friend's back. "That's right. Scotty here would like to get himself a *Hustler*. It's been a long time since we've been out hunting for beaver. Ain't that right, Scotty?"

Mansoor normally would have asked for ID, but he did not want any trouble. He had smelled alcohol on their breaths. Mansoor removed a bundle of keys from his jacket pocket and unlocked the drawer under the counter. "There you go," he said, and slapped the magazine onto the glass counter.

The Hulk flipped through the pages with titles like "Bigger and Better Juggs" across the top. He laughed. "A jug o' beer and a couple of jugs is all a man ever needs. Come on, Scotty, take a look at these."

Scotty snatched the magazine.

The Hulk pointed a thumb toward his friend. "See what happens when you deprive a man of life's pleasures for too long?"

A surge of anger rose in Mansoor's belly. Why the hell had he allowed Layla to push him into carrying such trash? Once, he had even examined the *poozee* magazines himself—slipped them into his jacket when he went to the washroom. They were filled with filth. He vowed to burn every single one as soon as these bastards left. He rang in the magazines and informed the men of their total.

The Hulk, his eyebrows knitted together, asked incredulously, "Holy Christ, you trying to rip us off or what?" He elbowed his friend. "Scotty, I think this here man is trying to rip us off."

"No, no. Not at all." Mansoor tore the receipt from the register and showed them the cost of each item. The Hulk swiped the receipt out of Mansoor's fingers. "What?" he said, examining the receipt. "Why the hell is the price of gas so high? Ain't supposed to be this high."

"Oh, well, you see, the nighttime price is slightly higher."

"Are you pulling my leg? Bad enough Trudeau's ripping us off and now you motherfucking niggers want to rob us high and dry too?"

The word *nigger* shocked Mansoor—not because he hadn't been called other names before, names like Paki. Paki, he could, in a way, understand. After all, he did look Indian or Pakistani—even if he wasn't. But *nigger* implied black. And my God, if there was one thing he wasn't, it was black! For this, Mansoor felt highly offended. Don't these bastards understand anything? He wanted to push up his sleeve, rub his skin, and show these men that he was brown. Brown, *madre-chod,* brown! Instead, Mansoor shovelled the items into a plastic bag and offered a solution. "Tell you what. Pay for the gas only. The rest of the items are on the house."

"Is that right? Well, that's awfully kind of you. But seeing that you're in such a generous mood," the Hulk slid the plastic bag back to Mansoor, "why don't you fill us up with a few more packets of Export A's?"

Scotty shook open a centrefold as Mansoor threw more packets of cigarettes into the bag. They better not ask for anything more. This was it! He would not tolerate being taken advantage of.

The Hulk's laughter rumbled through the store as he retrieved the bag from Mansoor. "Why, thank you very much. And here," he tugged the white pompom of his hat, "I'm supposed to be Santee Claus. Hey, Scotty, you need anything else? It ain't every day you meet a real fucking Santa Claus, eh?"

Scotty stuffed a few sticks of beef jerky down his sweatshirt.

"Come on now, Scotty, take a few more things, why don't ya? Mr. Claus here has been kind enough to open his workshop for us—we ought not to insult the man."

Scotty grinned. "How about another *Hustler?*"

"Please now. Enough is enough," Mansoor said more loudly than he had intended. "If you can please just pay and go." For a moment, he wished that he had listened to Layla and installed an alarm system.

"Come on, Scotty, let's get out of here. Looks like Santa's got his knickers in a knot." The men hooted with laughter and turned to leave.

"But wait. You haven't paid for the gas," Mansoor said, rushing behind them.

The men continued toward the front door. "Boo-hoo," responded the Hulk, rubbing his fists to his eyes. "Cry me a fucking river."

Mansoor felt a flood of heat rise from his belly. In his mind's eye, he was driving to the Sikh gurdwara with his house servant, Joseph, in the passenger seat of the Mercedes. The gurdwara was now the only safe haven for persons without status, people who belonged nowhere and who hadn't been able to get out before Amin's deadline. Mansoor stepped out of his car, taking his one suitcase with him, before he handed Joseph the keys—not just to his car but also to their house. The business was already gone. Soon after Layla and the children left for England, five army officers had stormed into one of his shops, brandishing machetes. They demanded money and the keys. Mansoor wanted to resist but he was overcome with an intense fear. It was as if he had been swimming leisurely at the Aga Khan Sports Club when he suddenly realized that he was not in a pool but in Lake Victoria. Bulging crocodile eyes surfaced all around him. Mansoor complied with the officers and quietly walked out of Govindji Visram and Sons, Inc.

No! Mansoor now said to himself. He would not let that happen again. All the things he had worked so hard for would not be taken away from him this time. He would not start over, yet again. How many generations would it take, he asked himself, before his family, his community, would have a permanent home instead of constantly leaving in search of a better life or being tossed out of one country or another, as if they were tennis balls in a political match? No! Canada would be different. Canada would be their permanent home. Mansoor knew he had no choice; he reached for the Hulk's shoulder and held on firmly.

"You can't go. You must pay."

The Hulk's fist whirled around, dropping Mansoor to his knees. Blood filled his mouth.

"Don't cause no trouble, old man. There's two of us here and only one of yous."

Get up, Mansoor told himself. Get up. You are Mansoor Visram Govindji. King of Kampala. Lightweight Champion. Master of Crocodiles. Mansoor shot up from his knees and punched as hard as he could. He only grazed the Hulk's chin.

The Hulk burst into laughter. "Come on, Santa. You really want to have a go at it?" He bounced up and down on the balls of his feet, his hands clenched into fists. "Floats like a butterfly, stings like a bee."

Layla, who had woken to go to the bathroom, pushed open the interconnecting door in time to see the Hulk delivering a final blow to Mansoor. "Stop!" she yelled, her firm voice ricocheting through the store.

The Hulk seemed to panic. He grabbed his friend's arm and the two of them scrambled outside.

"Get out," Mansoor whispered, his fingers on his bloody lips. He had fallen, once again, to his knees. "Get out of my store."

Layla rushed to double-bolt the door. From the front window, she then watched a dog jump back into the truck before the culprits screeched away. She rushed to Mansoor and reached down as far as her belly would allow, offering him her hand.

"No!" Mansoor raised his palm to her. "Leave me."

Layla walked to the back of the store and waited for him. She watched her husband struggle for a few moments before he finally stood up on his own. The Christmas lights strung on the Hawaiian mural twinkled in Mansoor's eyes. He marched to the wall, snatched handfuls of the green wires pinned to the palm tree and tore them down, taking strips of the mural off with it. He threw the fistful of jumbled lights and paper down and then walked slowly toward Layla. His pyjama sleeves had slipped out from his suit jacket. He wiped his mouth on the edge of a sleeve, covering it with blood.

"Don't worry," Layla said. She stood in the door frame and held the door open for him with an outstretched arm. "I'll do the laundry tomorrow."

Mansoor only nodded; his gaze was still fixed on the shop floor. But when he raised his head to her, he saw, as if for the first time, the outline of Layla's strong legs underneath her thin *kanga*, the flood of light from the house illuminating the shape of a body capable of bearing the weight of two.

Mansoor turned off the 24-hour sign and then stepped through the store–house door. Layla closed the door behind them and then together, they walked back into their house.

🐚 Baby Khaki's Wings

Baby Khaki was born with a set of transparent wings, which lay flat against her back, camouflaged against her milky brown skin. If you picked the baby up, laid her across your lap, and inspected her closely enough, perhaps ran your finger along the outline of her back, then maybe, just maybe, you might be able to feel a thin pipe—the frame of her wings. But even then, this was most difficult as it was easy to confuse this piping with a bulbous vein, ready to burst if the skin was slightly punctured. Across the width of Baby Khaki's back, between her shoulders, there was a thin slit—a pouch to tuck wings in. The tip of the right wing turned up toward the sky, but only ever-so-slightly, as if it was ready to be peeled off like the soft shell of an overcooked egg. No one learned about Baby Khaki's ability to fly until much, much later. Thankfully, the secret of her wings was guarded by her ayah, Aisha.

As with most Business People (and other Very Important People) in Tanzania, it was customary to hire an ayah for each child—not because it was always necessary but because ayahs were quite an affordable luxury, so much so that they became an expected expense line in many household budgets. Plus, many husbands reasoned, the presence of an ayah would not only ensure that each child received abundant care but also free their wives to focus on other extremely important duties: those of properly taking care of them.

The Khakis of Arusha had not been able to find a good ayah and Baby Khaki was due to arrive any day now. When Mr. Khaki told his brother in Zanzibar about their difficulty, his brother promptly offered to send their ayah, Aisha, to Arusha—as a loan of sorts. Mr. Khaki accepted and thanked his brother for what seemed, at that time, like a very generous gesture. He knew that his brother and sister-in-law had hired Aisha with the hope of having a child themselves—but after months of trying, his brother's wife had been unable to conceive.

Before leaving for Arusha, Aisha overheard the Khakis of Zanzibar discussing the lack of children in their household over tea on the verandah. They had tried all sorts of remedies to counter such bad luck, even leaving sacrifices for the spirits on the roof of the house, but nothing seemed to work. After some deliberation, they became convinced that Aisha was the source of their problems. After hiring her, hadn't their business taken a turn for the worse? Hadn't Mrs. Khaki fallen down the stairs and broken her ankle? (Poor thing!) And how about the time Mr. Khaki became very ill with some unknown sickness (and he had been unable to go to the shop for almost a fortnight!). And once, Mrs. Khaki had seen the ghost of a child partially emerge from the kitchen wall and then sink back into the plaster, as if caught between two worlds. It was Aisha, undoubtedly, who had ordered an *uganga* on them, rendering them childless. On top of that, they had also heard from several neighbours that Aisha had been seen returning from the bush late at night, and really, what kind of girl does that? Only a whore or someone up to no good. Worse yet, there had been many rumours lately about the increasing activities of the Wachawi. What if Aisha hadn't just ordered the spell but belonged to this secret sect and possessed the powers to evoke strong *juju* herself? They had to do something quickly. Otherwise their fates would be sealed!

They decided to test their suspicions by sending her to Arusha. If their suspicions proved to be correct, then it would serve as a double blessing: a child in their home and a slip in fortune for the Khakis of Arusha—rectifying a lifetime of misaligned stars favouring one brother over another.

Soon after Aisha left Zanzibar, Mrs. Khaki of Zanzibar conceived—trapping Aisha in Arusha. If she so much as placed a toe outside the prescribed path, then the Khakis of Arusha would surely send her back home to Zanzibar straight away, where rumours about her ominous powers would have already seeped and slithered their way into the gardens of other Very Important People. None of them would dare hire her again, not only in Stone Town but in all of Zanzibar. Then what would she do? Aisha had no family, no husband, and she would be thrown out on the street, alone once again.

Before she was hired by the Khakis of Zanzibar (who prided themselves on their charitable nature), Aisha had lived between the streets and the bush, doing whatever was required to survive. Aisha's father had remarried soon after his wife ran away with a young man from Oman, and when his new wife gave birth to a child of her own, she absolutely refused to keep Aisha any longer. Aisha's father felt trapped between his affections for his new, growing family and his unwavering love for his first child—no matter that she reminded him of the terrible insult from his former marriage. His inability to choose drove his new wife mad, so that there were daily arguments in the house, making life almost unbearable. In the end, Aisha's father apologized to his daughter and told her that he loved her very much, but he had no choice—she would have to leave.

It was the Thursday after the Khakis of Arusha brought their newborn daughter home from the hospital that Aisha discovered the perils of her new position. She walked into the baby's room to find Baby Khaki pushing her way out of her baby-hammock, wings unfurled, flapping vigorously, and her mouth sucking the air as if it was a flaccid breast, desperately trying to fill her belly.

At first, Aisha smiled and shook her head as a mother would when she finds her child in harmless mischief, but as Aisha stood on her tiptoes and plucked Baby Khaki out of the air—saving the baby from smashing her head against the ceiling—Aisha realized that the baby's deformity would most definitely be blamed on her. The Khakis of Arusha would blame her for casting an *uganga* on their daughter in the same way that the Khakis of Zanzibar had blamed her for the lack of children in their household. Her heart shook against her rib cage. Aisha held the baby close to her clattering heart, patted down the wings, and then tucked them into their pouch. Baby Khaki screamed and squirmed, throwing her head back and kicking Aisha in the stomach. Aisha let out a loud cry.

Hearing the mixture of Baby Khaki in distress and the ayah's scream, Mrs. Khaki rushed into the room. *"Kamanini sveze, bana, hanh?"* Mrs. Khaki yelled, and snatched Baby Khaki from Aisha. "What in God's name are you doing to my child?"

"Nothing, Mamma. I am doing nothing." Aisha twisted her hands in the pockets of her pinafore.

"Then why the hell is she crying like this? And why were you screaming at her? She is a baby for God's sake, not an animal. Such a good baby. Never cries like this, never fusses." Mrs. Khaki looked down and stroked Baby Khaki's head, but the baby continued to cry. *"Bas,* bheta, *bas.* It's all over now. No one is going to hurt you, okay? Don't worry, *mitu,* Mummy is here." Juggling the baby in one hand, Mrs. Khaki reached out and grabbed Aisha's arm, leaned in closer. "If I ever, ever find out you have done anything to my child, anything, by God, somebody better help you."

Aisha stepped back, her heart jammed. Mrs. Khaki pulled her arm with greater strength. "Count it your luck that this time I won't be telling Mr. Khaki. You think I'm upset—he wouldn't tolerate your *shenze-wara*—not for a second!" Mrs. Khaki dug her manicured nails into Aisha's arm before she flung it free from her grip.

Aisha's face felt hot. She wanted to yell and scream back, maybe even slap Mrs. Khaki hard across the cheek. Instead she cradled her strained arm across her body.

Mrs. Khaki reassured her baby once again, then handed her to Aisha. "Be careful! I don't want any more trouble." Mrs. Khaki checked her watch. "Feed her. It's time." She walked out of the baby's room, turned the corner, and ran straight into Mr. Khaki, who had just returned home from working at his newest venture, Khaki Arms & Ammunition.

"*Arrey,* watch yourself!" Mr. Khaki wrapped his fingers around Mrs. Khaki's shoulder, pushed her aside, and then removed the rifle that swung from his shoulder and leaned it against the wall.

Mrs. Khaki nodded and apologized; she sensed right away that her husband was in a foul mood. Must be all the stress from the new shop. Can't be easy working with those unreasonable tourists. And now with the onslaught of so many American hunters, it can only be harder. Mrs. Khaki felt great sympathy for her husband. Yes, she was a very lucky woman indeed, so very lucky to have a husband like Mr. Khaki—unlike the many, many other women who just did not seem capable of attracting good men. Poor souls! If only those women would volunteer for the community or do other charitable work, then good fortune would certainly be theirs.

Having noted Mr. Khaki's mood, Mrs. Khaki quickly changed the subject to one of his favourite topics: his daughter. "The baby is well. Eating plenty, *pani-pesab*—all good."

Mr. Khaki broke into a smile. "Good, good. Let me take a look."

Mrs. Khaki was pleased that she had been able to change her husband's mood. She asked Aisha to bring the baby out. Mr. Khaki placed his rifle in a scabbard lashed to the hall chair and then held his daughter at arm's length, let his glasses slip down his nose, and inspected his child. He glanced at his wife, then back at the baby. Yes, yes, she will be as beautiful as her mother. Thank God! And in that moment, Mr. Khaki felt great admiration for his wife. She was exquisite, wasn't she?

He remembered how he had been overwhelmed by her beauty right from the very start. When he announced his marriage plans to his mother, she screamed and yelled and told him that he was shameless for making marriage arrangements without consulting her first, and worse yet, he had chosen such an utterly lousy family. Bad enough the girl's father was in the lowly shoe business—this will bring nothing but bad luck, believe you me, and then to top it all off, their family is littered with so many imperfections, have you not noticed, son? Haven't you seen that cousin-brother with a club foot? Can't even walk. Or how about that auntie, you know, the fatty-fatty one—she has an extra pinky finger. Then there's that uncle's second wife, her child was fine and then one day, God knows why, she stopped talking. Just like that. Stopped right in mid-sentence. This must be the work of the devil only. And don't forget the older sister, hanh? She has skin the colour of *makara*. *Uh-ruh-ruh!* Are you mad, son? Please don't do it! I beg of you. You will only bring such bad, bad *bahati* into this good family of ours. It will make your poor dead father turn in his grave. Mr. Khaki's mother's pleas were futile, so she enlisted the help of others—cousins, uncles, and grandparents—to knock some sense into the boy. But nothing worked. Mr. Khaki ignored everybody's pleas; he didn't care one little bit what anybody said. All he knew was that he wanted this woman and he would have her. And now, as he stared at the beautiful baby his wife had produced for him, he was certain, absolutely certain, that he had made an excellent choice.

Mr. Khaki handed the baby back to Mrs. Khaki and asked her in Kutchi so that Aisha would not understand, "Everything good with the servant-girl?"

"Yes, yes. She's working out fine."

Mr. Khaki smiled, happy that his house was in order. In his head, he started to organize the tasks for the afternoon: first and foremost, unpack the shipment of .500 rifles that had arrived from Germany, get the servant-boy to clean and hang them properly on the rack (good merchandising, that's what the Americans liked, he had been told), and, ah yes, don't forget to put the new licence rate-card up on the window. (Thank goodness Tanzania Hunter had increased the General Game Licence cost to one hundred shillings!) Yes, yes, business will surely be good with all those rich Americans in town, ready and eager to check off all the animals on their lists. Mr. Khaki realized he had much to do before the new lot of Americans arrived and so he requested that his lunch be served right away. Mrs. Khaki nodded, passed the baby to Aisha, and then rushed downstairs to the kitchen.

Later that afternoon, during Mrs. Khaki's nap, Aisha quietly searched the hall closet, and returned to the baby's room with needles and a spool of brown thread. She lifted the baby out of her hammock, laid her across her lap, and fingered some Vicks VapoRub onto the wing-pouch. Aisha turned on the tape recorder, slipped in the newest collection of nursery rhymes, gently stuffed the baby's mouth with a small cloth, and dipped a needle into a bottle of Dettol.

BABY KHAKI'S POUCH remained sewn shut for months, until one day Aisha returned to the garden with some toys to find Baby Khaki caught in the branches of a small *machungwa* tree. The baby hung there, sucking her thumb, as if she were a ripe fruit ready to be picked. The weight of Aisha's spine pushed down into her legs. She scanned the courtyard to make sure the Khakis were still inside.

She grabbed a chair, climbed on, and reached up toward Baby Khaki—but the baby was out of her grasp. In a panic, she jumped off the chair, took the footstool from under the garden table, and placed it on top of the chair. She mounted the two-storey ladder she had created, wobbling on the uneven surface. She reached up on her tiptoes and rustled the branches until the baby tumbled out—breaking and bending a few branches so that leaves and even an orange hit Aisha below. Ouch! Aisha ignored the spray of foliage, but just as she seized the baby, the stool slipped from under her. She came tumbling down, landing on the grass with a *thud* and Baby Khaki on top of her. Aisha quickly stood up, dusted the baby off, and then crumpled up the baby's wings and tried to tuck them back into the frayed pouch. Baby Khaki let out a wail.

"Shh, shh, *toto*. Everything is fine." Aisha patted the baby. "Please stop your crying." Baby Khaki continued. "Stop it!" Aisha squeezed the baby hard. She looked up and saw Mrs. Khaki pushing open the bedroom window.

Mrs. Khaki leaned out, her voice hurled down into the garden and rolled into the wild bush trail behind the house to the base of Mount Meru. "What's all the *kelele* about? What the hell are you doing down there?"

Aisha held the baby closer, and rocked back and forth, almost losing her balance again. "Mamma, she is crying for food. Look, I am feeding her." She reached into her dress for her breast, cradled the baby closer, and shoved the breast deep into the baby's mouth. The baby refused at first, continuing to cry.

"Don't make me come down there. You are paid very, very nicely—and what all for, if I always have to keep on checking on you!"

Aisha pushed her breast harder into the baby's mouth and whispered, "Drink, child-of-Satan, drink!" Baby Khaki bit Aisha's nipple. Aisha held her breath. She knew this was the baby's sign that she would now start sucking. Baby Khaki wrapped her mouth around Aisha's breast and pulled her milk out.

"See, Mamma," Aisha said, half smiling, pointing at the baby. "Everything, it's *mzuri-sana.*"

Mrs. Khaki shook her head, closed the window, and turned away.

AISHA WAS DESPERATE to find a solution to stop Baby Khaki from flying. She had no choice. She had to cut the wings off! Aisha sterilized a pair of scissors and then set about preparing the baby. She slipped her fingers into the wing-pouch and pulled each wing out. Some white fluff flew out. Aisha smoothed out the creases on the wings and laid them across the baby's back. Only then did she realize that the wings had changed: they were now lightly downed with golden-brown hair. Aisha stroked the wings—they were so soft! What a beautiful baby! She picked up the baby and tossed her into the air. The baby cooed and floated back into Aisha's arms. Aisha laughed and kissed the baby all over her chubby cheeks. What a sweet, sweet child! Aisha threw the baby up again. Baby

Khaki giggled, flapped her wings, and flew directly toward the open window.

"Oh, *toto!*" Aisha ran after the baby, arms high above her. "Come back, *toto*. Come back!"

The baby was partly outside the window when Aisha reached out, caught an ankle and pulled, but a gust of wind spun around the baby like a silkworm and sucked her out even farther. Aisha held on, determined to pull the baby back inside—but the current was so strong that it lifted Aisha off the floor, so that together the ayah and the baby formed a straight line up—like balloons tied to the house to mark a celebration. For a moment, Aisha felt so light that she wanted to be completely lifted up and away, but as she continued to rise, panic filled her and she was reminded of the task at hand. She quickly curled her feet under the inside ledge of the window and tethered herself to the house. Eventually the wind let up, releasing both of them. They tumbled and collapsed onto the bedroom floor, Baby Khaki on top of Aisha.

When Aisha regained her composure and stood to straighten herself out, she realized how foolish she had been: This devil-child is toying with me, trying to win the affections of my heart! No, she wouldn't have it anymore. She wasn't that gullible. Aisha was more determined than ever to stop the baby from flying. This was too risky! She had to cut the baby's wings off *maramoja*.

Aisha laid the baby on the cot, lifted one wing off the baby's back, and carefully placed the tip of the scissors at the apex of the wings. Her hands trembled—this was no easy task, amputating a baby's wings. But she had to do it. She made the first tear. A watery substance oozed from the wound, trickled down the baby's back, and then dripped onto the cot. Aisha looked away. Please, God, save me. What am I doing? What has become of me that I can harm an innocent child? Aisha shook these thoughts out of her head and continued. More water gushed out as the scissors made their way down the first wing. No! *Hapana!* She threw the scissors on the floor. No! She wouldn't do this. She couldn't do it. She wasn't a monster. Aisha licked her finger and applied it to the torn wing, then leaned down and kissed the wound. She would have to find another solution, one that was not as barbaric.

A FEW DAYS LATER Aisha heard rumours that a Zanzibari witch doctor had recently moved to Arusha, and she decided to investigate. She discovered that the witch doctor, Mamma Zulekha, lived on Old Moshi Road, just a few streets over. Maybe, just maybe, Aisha prayed, this *waganga* would help her. Aisha made arrangements to take the baby to Mamma Zulekha while the Khakis were at the *mukhi's* house for their weekly game of *karata*.

Mamma Zulekha was an old, old woman with a small wrinkled face, bloodshot eyes, and a shaven head. She wore a long white robe that was speckled with red dots. She welcomed Aisha and motioned for her to follow her to the *shamba* in the back and sit near a small fire. Aisha undressed the baby and placed her on Mamma Zulekha's lap.

Mamma Zulekha rubbed her head. "Yes, yes, I have heard of this phenomenon before. She is like big insect, hanh?" She laughed as she picked at Baby Khaki's wings. "But, *weh,* it is too unusual for such a little baby to have learned the craft *fatafut,* oh-so-quickly—especially when she is landlocked. In Zanzibar or Pemba, I understand—the island winds can help the child on its first flight, carry it for miles upon miles until a messenger of Shatan claims it. But in this case, I don't understand." Mamma Zulekha paused. "Oh-yo, this can only mean that the baby has extra-special powers! I am certain of it—we must act very quickly. This *uganga* has been cast by a very strong *djinn.*"

Aisha folded her arms, cupping her elbows in her palms. "Why, Mamma Zulekha, why must I endure so much suffering while others enjoy such worry-free lives? I have done nothing to deserve such a fate. Nothing at all. I am a God-fearing woman. I have had a difficult life, Mamma, but I have never complained. I have never asked for too much and yet this is what is served to me!"

Mamma Zulekha nodded. "Yes, my child, we all are deserving of a good life, but you must have done something to generate so much ill will. Make no mistake, life is not so random."

Aisha hung her head.

Mamma Zulekha reached across the fire and stroked her face. "Perhaps it is a simple matter, child. It could be that somebody is jealous of your beauty and has ordered this curse."

Aisha pushed Mamma Zulekha's hand away. "Or it could be the mother's fault! She is the one who has not taken all the normal precautions of preventing such deformities. I watch her. She is very careless—clipping her nails after sundown, taking evening baths, walking under trees even when she has her monthlies. It is her stupidity that has invited Shatan's congregation into their house. She is asking for trouble! Yet I will be the one who ends up paying for her actions!" Aisha pounded her fists on her thighs. "Please, Mamma Zulekha, I beg you. Please help me. You are the only one who knows about my troubles. I am new in this town and cannot afford for anyone, not anyone, to know my secret. I am willing to do whatever it takes to stop this baby from flying."

Mamma Zulekha hesitated. "Yes, anything is possible, child." She rubbed her hands vigorously over the fire and placed her palms on her eyelids. She then shrouded herself and the baby with a white sheet. At first, Mamma Zulekha rocked back and forth, but soon she began shaking and speaking in an incomprehensible language. Aisha instinctively stood up, ready to run. But suddenly Mamma Zulekha sprang up and the sheet slipped off her. Sweat covered her brow and dripped down her face. Mamma Zulekha held Baby Khaki in outstretched hands. "Yes, yes, I have a solution. I must see this baby daily for forty days in order to rid her of her ailment. This is the only way. The remedy will not work otherwise."

"Forty days, Mamma? Dear God, how will I do that? I cannot get away from the *bwana*'s house for forty days." Aisha wrung the fabric of her dress around her finger. "Can I not administer the remedy myself?"

Mamma Zulekha let out a belly laugh and shook her head.

Aisha slumped down to the ground. "I don't know what else to do, Mamma. My life depends on this."

Mamma Zulekha touched Aisha's head. "You can apply the medicine, but your touch may well take forty years. My mother was a witch doctor, and her mother before that. Training is possible, but it can take years upon years. Such an intricate craft cannot just be learned overnight."

Aisha burst into tears. "I have no family, no husband. Where will I go when they throw me out on the street?"

"Calm down, child, calm down. Let me think for one moment." Mamma Zulekha reached for a cup, and after taking a long slurp, she closed her eyes. A few minutes later, she opened them. "Okay, okay. This is what you will do. I will brew an extra-strong remedy for the child. There will be some risk—but it has to be strong-*kama*-strong to offset the weakness in your touch. It is not the prescribed remedy, but it seems there is no other way."

Aisha stood up and rushed to Mamma Zulekha. "We have a solution!"

"But I warn you," Mamma Zulekha wagged her finger, "the welfare of the child will be in your hands entirely."

"Yes, yes, Mamma, that is fine."

Mamma Zulekha nodded and walked to the lone baobab tree. The tree had hundreds of nails hammered into its trunk and even more shreds of cloth hanging from its branches. She asked Aisha to hold the baby against the trunk, and then Mamma Zulekha pricked the baby under her arms and collected drops of blood on a silver tray. Strangely, the baby did not cry.

"The remedy will take some days to produce. I will come and apply the first round. You will see what I do and then follow this plan daily for forty days, at the prescribed hour—one hour before sundown."

"Yes! Yes! It will work, I know it." Aisha clapped her hands.

"Don't remain so confident," Mamma Zulekha warned. "You will tempt Shatan to counter your strength."

"You are so wise. Of course. I will contain myself." Aisha hugged Mamma Zulekha.

Aisha paid Mamma Zulekha the pre-negotiated sum of money and they arranged a time for their next visit.

That evening, Aisha slipped a thin sisal cord around Baby Khaki's ankle and tied it to her wrist. She would use this temporary solution until Mamma Zulekha's concoction started to work.

MAMMA ZULEKHA ARRIVED as planned on the following Friday when the Khakis were at jamatkhana for their evening prayers. She carried a large bowl and several small sacks.

"Come, Mamma, this way. We have to hurry, I don't want the neighbours to see." Aisha waved Mamma Zulekha through the garden gate. They rushed upstairs to the baby's room.

Aisha took Baby Khaki out of her hammock and placed her on the floor. The baby cooed. Aisha reached down and slipped the sisal cord off the baby's ankle but kept it dangling from her wrist like a frayed umbilical cord.

Mamma Zulekha turned the child to face east. "Watch and listen carefully, my child."

Aisha kneeled next to Mamma Zulekha. First, Mamma Zulekha performed a silent prayer, touched the baby's head, then each hand, her stomach, and each foot. She lit some incense and waved it over the baby's body. She tapped several herbs onto a silver tray, then reached into the top of her robe and removed a vial containing the baby's blood. Using her fingers, she mixed the blood with the herbs, then flipped Baby Khaki onto her stomach and daubed medicine on the wings. She applied most of the remedy to the crux of the wings at the base of the baby's neck, where the wings were fastened, and on the pouch opening, the thin slit between the baby's shoulder blades. Mamma Zulekha recited a prayer five times and called on the demons.

"Do not be angry with us, we will do all we can. To those who belong to the house of God, may they have mercy on you by their favour, and we ask of your pardon. Have pity on us and remove our terrible suffering. Pity her in whom you are, and forgive her with all forgiveness, because those who forgive die pious. Forgive us our sins, forgive, forgive, in the name of all true believers." Mamma Zulekha sprinkled a bottle of rosewater all over the baby and then spread her palm across the middle of the baby's back.

"These wings shall get softer and softer and fall off after forty days, God-willing."

Aisha heard the front gate opening and the familiar sound of the Khakis' white Audi. "Mamma, you must go. Hurry. They cannot find you here."

"Burn some incense, otherwise they will smell the remedy. And do not forget to put an offering on the roof each night. Now, go take care of the baby. I know my way out." Mamma Zulekha cradled Aisha's head in her hands. "Many blessings. Let us pray that the demons co-operate."

"Thank you! Thank you." Aisha held Mamma Zulekha by the waist. "I am indebted to you forever."

Mamma Zulekha smiled. "No need to be so thankful. First, let us see if the altered remedy works—that is the important thing." She waved goodbye and quickly shuffled out the door.

After Aisha lit some sandalwood incense and pushed the bowl and sacks of medicine under her cot, she picked up Baby Khaki, wrapped her in a blanket, and placed her in the baby-hammock. She then sat down on a chair and hummed a nursery rhyme as she gently swung the baby. Aisha pinched the last remaining ray of light from the setting sun between her thumb and baby finger and slipped it into her mouth, let it sit there, trapped under her tongue. She laid her head back and curled her calves under the seat, letting her soft brown body ease into the chair.

That night, Aisha dreamt she was pregnant. A nightingale pecked her plump belly, trying to crack it open. The baby wailed inside her, aching, it seemed, to get out. But just before the baby popped its head out and took its first breath, Aisha bolted up in bed. When she calmed herself down and was about to fall back to sleep, she heard what seemed like a bird flapping away through the open window.

EACH EVENING, one hour before sunset, Aisha administered the remedy exactly as prescribed. After each application, she would poke at the baby's wings—testing them as if she were testing the flakiness of *mandazi*. Each night, the wings became visibly weaker, so that soon they were quite limp—as if they had been soaked in a washtub overnight. By the ninth night, when Aisha prodded the wings, she created a puncture the size of her index finger in the wings. Aisha smiled as she peeled the skin of the baby's wing off her finger. Thank God, the prescription is working! Aisha would have to visit Mamma Zulekha soon to express her thanks. Aisha felt a surge of confidence; the end was near. She would soon be released from the terrible burden of hiding these wings. This sudden sense of freedom made Aisha laugh out loud. She had never been happier, had never felt lighter in her life. Her laughter spread like a bushfire, shooting up through her throat, filling her mouth, and finally bursting through her lips. She laughed so intensely that she eventually collapsed to the floor, rolling all over the room, intoxicated by this new feeling of freedom. When Aisha finally came to, she was completely exhausted and fell asleep immediately.

As she slept, she dreamt that she was walking in and out of the corridors of Stone Town, but strangely, all the streets were deserted. The vendors had closed their shops and there were no schoolchildren to be seen, even though Aisha could hear the muffled voice of a child counting: *moja, mbili, tatu,* ready or not, here I come! She could also hear children scampering here and there, as if they were right next to her, but there was no one in sight—all of them, it seemed, were tucked away in the various *gulleys* and gutters of Stone Town. But Aisha could feel the children watching her. She stopped, snapped back around, hoping to catch a glimpse of one. But nothing. She was alone. She kneeled down and looked under the fish vendors' stalls, peered into the tailor's shop. Nothing. Where were they all? Just then, the muezzin's voice bellowed over a loudspeaker with the call for prayers and the sky opened its belly. Water gushed out, pouring down on Zanzibar with such intensity that the island was lifted from the earth, eventually bobbing up and down in rainwater, just under the surface of the sky.

BY THE THIRTEENTH NIGHT, to Aisha's horror, Baby Khaki's wings started to get stronger, not softer! At first, Aisha ignored this change, chalking it up to the nuances of the prescription, but by the sixteenth night, Aisha became extremely worried and frustrated. Why wasn't this remedy working? What had gone wrong? She was following the prescription exactly as ordered. Aisha decided that perhaps the solution was to apply more and more of the concoction on the wings. But it soon became apparent that the more she applied, the stronger the wings became, so that they became harder and harder to fold and tuck into their pouch. Once, they just popped straight out of the pouch as if they were breasts being pushed into a dress too small. Without thinking, Aisha reached for the scissors, but the baby slipped out of her arms and flew around the room creating a grand ruckus as she hit the walls and the closed windows. Aisha chased the baby back and forth across the room and finally cornered her. She pulled Baby Khaki down and then laid her on the cot, where she placed her knee firmly against the baby's back, and reached, once again, for the scissors. Aisha was so preoccupied with the task at hand that she did not hear Mrs. Khaki walking up the stairs toward the baby's room.

"What are you doing?" Mrs. Khaki screamed, rushing toward her baby.

Aisha stood up immediately. "Mamma?"

Mrs. Khaki snatched the baby up from the cot. "*Suno,* husband, *suno!*" she yelled at the top of her lungs. "Call the doctor!" Mrs. Khaki turned to Aisha. "You devil-woman. *Kumamayao!*" She dispensed a solid slap across Aisha's face. "What have you done? What have you done to my baby?" Mrs. Khaki cried and screamed, tears rushing out, ruining her makeup, as she continued to inspect her baby. "What is this?" She tentatively poked the wings. "Answer me, *bhenchod!* What have you done to my baby?"

"Nothing, Mamma, nothing. The baby: she flies."

"What are you talking about?" Mrs. Khaki's legs were shaking so much that she had to lay the baby back down on the cot. She then collapsed to the floor, patting the baby gently. "Husband!" she whimpered. "Please hurry up. The baby is hurt."

Aisha grabbed the baby from under Mrs. Khaki's hands. She cupped the child in her hands and held her up to the ceiling. "Look, Mamma, the baby, she flies." Aisha released Baby Khaki upward, blowing at her like an eyelash for a wish, but the baby just fluttered her wings briefly, then tumbled down onto the cot, weakened, perhaps, from the earlier chase.

Mrs. Khaki snatched her child from Aisha. "Have you gone mad?"

Just then, Mr. Khaki rushed into the room and discovered his wife and daughter in this terrible state.

"Look, look what the servant-girl has done to our child." Mrs. Khaki displayed the baby's back to her husband.

Mr. Khaki erupted with shock and anger. "*Pisha Mowla!* What in God's name has happened to my child?"

"This is the work of the devil!" Mrs. Khaki was barely able to lift her arm, but she pointed to Aisha. "And she is the devil's messenger!"

Aisha felt limp with exhaustion—as if she had been purged of all her energy. "No, Mamma. I am a God-fearing woman. Please, spare me. I have done my best to take care of this child."

"You will pay for this!" Mr. Khaki told Aisha in an even but harsh tone. "You will never work anywhere in Tanzania, or for the matter, Zanzibar. Nowhere! You will wish you were dead."

"Please, *bwana,* please forgive me. I beg of you. Despite all my efforts, I was unable to ward off the spirits."

"So you admit it? You admit your liaison with Shatan himself?"

Aisha felt cornered. She had nothing and nobody to fall back on, and although she knew the purity of her actions, she felt she had no choice but to repent. Aisha looked down. "Yes, sir, I admit it. Please have mercy on me!"

Mr. Khaki felt reasonably satisfied with the confession and delighted that he would now have a greater amount of negotiating power over her. "You will have to pay for your mistakes."

"Yes, sir, I will do anything you ask. Please, I only ask that you give me another chance."

Mr. Khaki looked at his wife to gauge her reaction, but she was still distraught and had not absorbed any of the conversation. Mr. Khaki shook his head and wondered why it had taken his wife this long to discover that a terrible spell had been cast on their child. What the hell had she been doing with her time? He looked at Baby Khaki and noticed she wasn't even wearing *anjar* under her eyes. He turned the child's ear down. No *anjar* there, either! For God's sake, his wife hadn't taken any of the normal precautions to ward off evil! Did she not possess any common sense? As he looked at Mrs. Khaki, still sitting on the floor with her head on the edge of the cot, hair dishevelled, face smudged with makeup, he wondered for the first time if he should have listened to his mother's warning about the terrible luck in his wife's family. Yes, she was beautiful, but in the end, she had still produced a deformed child for him and no amount of beauty could outweigh this fact. Perhaps he should have considered other qualities when he was choosing a wife.

Mr. Khaki walked over to his wife, leaned down, and slapped her. "Useless bitch."

Mrs. Khaki was in such a daze that she hardly even felt the sting across her face. It was as though this new knowledge about her life, the idea that something this terrible could happen to her, to her of all people, broke her like a wooden spoon across a knee, and paralyzed her. "Why me? Why me?" was all she could utter.

Mr. Khaki turned his gaze to Aisha. "You will have to pay for the rest of your life—you understand?"

"Yes, sir. I understand."

Mr. Khaki explained to Aisha that from now on she would have to report to him and that he would be the one to give her instructions with regard to the baby's care. As well, he would make prompt arrangements for the surgical removal of Baby Khaki's wings.

Aisha recoiled as she remembered her own barbaric attempt at cutting off the baby's wings. No! Aisha thought. "Please, *bwana*, do not cut them off." Aisha picked up the baby from the cot and held her tightly against her breast.

A flicker of heat shot straight up Mr. Khaki's body and flushed his face. How dare she give me instructions on how to run my house! His arms reached out and pried the baby away from Aisha. He doubled the baby over his arm like a sack of rice, folded a wing, and ripped if off, then and there, like a page in a book.

The baby wailed. Aisha reached out and let the amputated wing land like a leaf on her palm.

Mr. Khaki held the baby toward Aisha in outstretched arms. "This, this is your bloody fault!"

The weight of the wing on Aisha's palm gave her a sudden conviction. She yelled loudly and clearly, "No! This is not my fault!" She grabbed the baby back from Mr. Khaki and ran straight out of the room.

Mr. Khaki could not believe the audacity of this servant-girl! He ran after her, determined to teach her a good lesson. He turned the corner and pursued her down the stairs, but then his eyes caught the scabbard lashed on the hall chair and he smiled, certain that no servant-girl would ever outsmart him. He returned to the bedroom and waited by the window.

Mr. Khaki heard a door being inched open and, soon enough, he saw Aisha running across the garden, the baby tucked in a *kanga* wrapped across her body. Mr. Khaki pushed open the window with his fingertips and aimed. Aisha ducked behind the *machungwa* tree, waited a moment, then ran again. Another shot and she jumped into the lavender bushes, then behind the jacaranda, running and hiding, running and hiding, past anything and everything in her way, straight toward the bush trail.

The baby's wing snapped out of the *kanga* like the sail of a dhow, and as Aisha ran, the baby bobbed up and down, faster and faster, until both of them whirred like a motor and lifted off the ground. As they rose, the wind generated a new wing from the scar of the old and Baby Khaki flapped her wings with a new fervour as she clawed her way out of the *kanga*. Mr. Khaki saw them rise above the forest and promptly fired again and again until he exhausted all his bullets. He then watched, with great satisfaction, as Aisha fell, arms spread, gently striking the tops of several cedar trees before disappearing into the dense bush below. Baby Khaki circled the trees, then dove like a duck into water. She resurfaced several times before they emerged together, Aisha folded in two, Baby Khaki mounted on Aisha's back, pulling her up toward the sky.

Bombshell Beauty

Presenting Amir Merchant, Future Son-in-Law

In order for Amir Merchant to take his fiancée, Zarina Jivraj, to the Grand Opening of the Pomegranate Ballroom, he had to ask her father's permission. Mr. Jivraj was hesitant; he was worried not only because it might spoil his good name but also because he knew very well what boys were like, so he refused.

Mrs. Jivraj shot her husband a dirty look as she spooned more *biryani* into Amir's plate. "Let them go now. It's the big opening of Amir's club. Plus all the youngsters are going everywhere these days."

Zarina, who sat next to her younger sister, Najma, laced her fingers into a tight knot on her lap and looked at her father.

Please say yes, Pappa! Zarina could hardly wait to be in the arms of her handsome new fiancé.

Up until now, there had been no place for the young people in Dar es Salaam to dance. The British Gymkhana was clearly off limits—not only for the Africans (obviously) but for them as well—except on the rare occasion that the District Commissioner sent invitations for his charitable and fundraising events to some of the well-to-do Asians. Amir's father had received one such invitation but had ripped it up on the spot. "Bastards! As if we need them so badly." He decided then and there that he would open a ballroom for the young people in his community. "Let them enjoy as well." Plus, he had said, it would be an excellent source of additional revenue for his growing empire. As soon as the Merchants announced the opening of the ballroom, all the young people in Dar es Salaam started making plans: new dresses and suits were made and purchased, there were lineups outside Shivji Shoe Shop & Repair, hair appointments were booked, and many spent their evenings practising popular dance steps from recent American films with stars like Lana Turner, Ava Gardner, and Rita Hayworth.

People often told Zarina that she looked just like Rita—as if she were a bombshell who'd stepped out of the screen at the Empire Theatre and onto the streets of Dar es Salaam. Even when she was a little girl, uncles, aunties, and cousins would follow her around, practically fighting to play with her or have her sit on their laps. It was as if she were a roll of Life Savers and they all wanted a piece. "Save her for my boy," aunties would say to her mother, who would beam with pride. "No, no. My boy would be much better," another auntie would pipe in. "Aye, if only I was younger," an uncle would counter. "What a bombshell beauty you are!" Zarina would just smile at their comments, but for some reason, she felt rotten, as if she were a fruit that was spoiled on the inside.

Mr. Jivraj tapped his hand on his plate, but several grains of rice stubbornly stuck to his fingers. "Who's saying no, Kulsum? If everyone else allows their children to jump in front of a train, does that mean we do the same? Besides," he clucked his tongue, "all these youngsters going everywhere these days are married youngsters, not engaged youngsters like our Zarina and Amir." He rolled his fingers around the outside of his plate, scooped the remaining rice into his hand, and muttered, "Why not speak when you know what you are speaking about?"

Mrs. Jivraj was not at all put off. Her topmost concern was appeasing her future son-in-law and ensuring that nothing, absolutely nothing, went wrong before the wedding. After all, this was no ordinary boy. This was Amir Merchant, one and only son of Hasanali S. Merchant, number one businessman in the whole of Tanganyika! Mrs. Jivraj did a mental inventory of all the things the Merchants owned: a biscuit factory upcountry, a coffee farm in Arusha, and here in Dar es Salaam, a toy shop, a spices shop, a pawnbroker's, a liquor store, a mattress shop, and now this ballroom. My God, did her husband have nails in his head? Did he not understand that they had to do their utmost to keep this boy happy? Of course their Zarina could get any boy she wanted with her extra good looks, but why had they refused all those proposals, made her wait until this late age of twenty to marry? Think, husband-*sala,* think for once in your life!

"Auntie, the food is excellent." Amir smiled at Mrs. Jivraj, then popped an onion slice into his mouth.

"Oh, I'm so happy you're enjoying." See what a good boy he is? Mrs. Jivraj shifted the skirt of her A-shaped dress, which was patterned with tiny red roses, and glanced at her younger daughter, Najma, stooped over her food, eating. Not like that one is going to be able to bring home a gem like Amir. This boy will help us change our lives. Thank God for Zarina! Not even married yet and Mr. Merchant had already made a generous offer to help Mr. Jivraj expand their *kanga* shop. After all these years, her good-for-nothing husband still had only one shop, while so many others were expanding and had money coming out of their *khand.* Mrs. Jivraj sat down and pulled her chair up to the table, her large breasts pressing against the edge. Her quick mind developed another option. "But if we send Najma along, it should be fine, nuh? Let her have a nice time too."

Najma, who had kept her eyes averted all evening, looked up from her plate, hoping desperately that her father would say yes. She made sure that she did not look at her future brother-in-law. Oh! He was so very good-looking with his fair skin and his big, *gul-gul* eyes. Why did Zarina always get everything she wanted? Ever since she was a little girl, Najma knew that she wasn't very pretty. Aunties and uncles would pat her on her head and then clamour to Zarina, eager to be the first to lift her onto their laps, pinch her cheeks, run their hands down her long, dark hair, and tell her how pretty she was. "So pretty, I just want to eat you up," people would say, nuzzling their mouths to her neck and shaking their heads vigorously. Once, when Shokat Uncle returned from a business trip to London with gifts for everyone, she saw him slip Zarina an extra bar of Cadbury's Dairy Milk. That night, Najma found half the chocolate bar under her pillow and although she wanted so much to eat it, she returned it to Zarina right away with a note: "I am not charity." It all seemed so unfair. She had always felt beautiful inside with the many wondrous thoughts running inside her, but her appearance seemed to betray her. If only, Najma thought, she could turn herself inside out, then people would flock to her the way they flocked to Zarina. But Najma refused to feel sorry for herself. One day I will find my prince, a man who will see me for who I am. Then everything will be different.

Mr. Jivraj held a green chili to his mouth, about to snap the tip. Instead, he put it down on his plate and looked at his wife. She always insisted on dragging matters out, but in this case, she had proposed a reasonable solution, hadn't she? So why not? What harm could come from one evening? "Both sisters will accompany you, Amir."

Amir hurried to swallow the food he was chewing; it slipped down his throat like a mouse down a snake. "Very good, Uncle."

Najma could barely contain herself. She was going to spend an evening at the Pomegranate Ballroom! She didn't mean to, but blurted out, "I can't wait to dance."

Mr. Jivraj placed both elbows on the table, leaned in, and looked sternly at her. "*Arrey, Najma*," he coughed as he glanced at his wife, "who said anything about dancing?"

Mrs. Jivraj wagged her finger at Najma. "Exactly, *junglee-salee.* You heard Pappa. Best to sit and watch. Go-*kama,* but only to keep your sister company. *Bas.* Finished talking." Why was this girl such a headache? Mrs. Jivraj was sick and tired of always having to worry about Najma. Bad enough the girl wasn't all that attractive—that sort of thing can be corrected somewhat. Hadn't she spent countless hours scrubbing Najma's dark skin with Vim and applying petroleum jelly nightly on her unruly hair? And no doubt, she had definitely improved some. Not bad at all really, but still, she was nothing at all like her sister. *Loi-peeyathi,* she drinks my blood, she would say to the aunties over a cup of tea and loud enough so that Najma could hear. But more than that, Najma was difficult to control from the very beginning. Even when she was only this high, she would run around with her dress over her head during prayers at jamatkhana. What to do with a girl like that? Her father wouldn't let me touch her—otherwise I would have beaten some sense into her. But one time, *weh.* I had no choice. Found her in the bathroom with a doll between her

legs! *Pisha Mowla.* What kind of animal had I given birth to? Is
this the way for a girl to behave? Exactly! So what else to do but
put my slippers to good use? But I had no chance. The shameless
girl ran straight out of the flat and into the courtyard. Naked!
What would the neighbours say? I tried my level best to catch
her; ran after her like a servant chasing a chicken. But I tell you,
it was impossible. Who knew a hippo could run so fast, hanh? I
had no choice; I woke her father from his afternoon nap. Told
him everything. But what did the *laloo* do? He caught her all
right, but instead of doing what any man would do, he just
stood there, trembling like a leaf. Bastard. "How else will she
learn her lesson?" I yelled. Finally, he gave her a solid slap across
the face and she let out a big fat scream. "Yes! That's it," I told
him. "That will teach her all right." But the idiot pulled away,
tears in his eyes. Tears, can you believe? The girl never cried
once and here was this grown man crying like a little baby.
Then, just like that, he disappeared into his office. From then
on, I knew for certain that I would have to handle all the affairs
in the household. I grabbed the girl and gave her a few good
ones, but soon enough, she slipped out of my grip and ran
away. Believe you me, if her father had straightened her out
then, we wouldn't have the problems we have today.

Zarina tucked the tips of her fingers under her thighs. Please,
don't spoil everything, Najma. Zarina hoped that her little sister
would not storm off to her room or create some sort of kafuffle,
as she so often did, in order to protest their parents' restrictions.

My God, what in the world would Amir think—her family were hooligans? Why can't Najma just behave herself? Doesn't she realize that tonight is of utmost importance? Why can't she think of anybody else but herself? When they were little, things were so different. Najma would follow Zarina around like a shadow and often insist that they sleep together. On those nights, they would stay up, whispering and giggling with hands over their mouths, pretending to be film stars in movies like *The Lady from Shanghai,* in which Najma played Orson Welles, a rogue hero who saves Rita Hayworth, played by Zarina, from thieves in Central Park. But then, as if overnight, Najma refused to have anything to do with Zarina—whether it was her offers to apply nail polish, style her hair, or just talk (like all sisters did) about delicious topics such as the boys they would most like to marry. Instead, Najma would shut Zarina out of their bedroom by propping a chair under the knob. "What have I done wrong?" Zarina once asked their mother. "Why is she so mean to me?" "Don't worry, bheta," Mrs. Jivraj said before she forced open the door. "Your sister, she's the jealous type, you see. What can you do if God has bestowed you with such beauty, hanh?"

Zarina leaned over to Najma, keen to soften her up for Amir's sake. "Come on, Najma, we'll dress up like princesses. It'll be so much fun. You can wear anything of mine that you want."

Najma looked at Zarina and, to Zarina's surprise, her mouth widened into a smile. "Even your new dress?"

No! Not that dress. That's the one she was planning to wear. Oh, that's okay, Zarina told herself. She'd have another dress made before the Grand Opening. Besides, once I'm married, when will Najma ever have a chance to go anywhere? Zarina prayed that her sister would develop a more amiable personality so that she too would have a normal life one day: a good husband, a nice house, and the joys of motherhood. Poor Najma! It was her duty, Zarina felt, to rise above her little sister's antics and set a good example for her. That was the only way Najma would learn. "Of course you can wear my dress."

It was all set then. They were going to the Grand Opening of the Pomegranate Ballroom. Najma filled with a nervous excitement as she imagined herself in Zarina's long black Rita Hayworth dress that Amir had purchased for her in London. Yes. She'll wear a long scarf and practise walking in heels and maybe, just maybe, she'll look as beautiful as Zarina does when she wears it. No, she'll look even more beautiful! She'll look like a star and all the boys will line up to dance with her.

Amir didn't say anything, but why the hell did he have to take Najma along? She would ruin the evening, following them everywhere like a dirty shadow. He wanted to have his beautiful fiancée on his arm without any encumbrances whatsoever. The whole bloody point of coming for this God-forsaken meal was to ensure that Zarina would be allowed to spend the evening with him, at his club, with his friends and colleagues. Good God, hadn't his family made enough gestures of goodwill to these people? Even offering her father investment capital to expand that shoddy store of his? He had been waiting months to be alone with this girl—this girl that every single boy in Dar wanted but was now officially his.

Behind the Scenes of the Prince and the Showgirl

Amir left soon after dinner in order to attend to a business matter. Mr. Jivraj was in excellent spirits, knowing that Zarina was marrying such a good fellow, that he decided to take the family for ice cream. They piled into his gleaming white Peugeot and as they headed toward Ocean Drive, Mr. Jivraj turned on the radio. His favourite song from the film *Mughal-e-Azam* boomed from the speakers. He tapped his fingers on the dashboard and sang along, *Ghunt ghunt kariiyu marna kyaa. Why die slowly in small choked breaths?* Mrs. Jivraj, who had already laid her head back on the seat, immediately leaned forward and turned down the volume. The car burrowed through the winding road and when they reached Oyster Bay, Mr. Jivraj pulled into the gravel parking lot where rows of African vendors were lined up with oil lamps offering *mogo* doused with lemon and chili, sticks of spicy *mishkaki,* and vanilla ice cream from steel drums. Mr. Jivraj and Najma jumped out of the car. Mrs. Jivraj refused to come out. She said her heels would sink into the sand and she certainly wasn't going barefoot. Zarina stayed back to keep her company.

Najma delivered the ice-cream cones to the car, then ran back to her father, who had, by then, walked to the water's edge; his shoes dangled from his fingers, waves lapped his feet. Mr. Jivraj felt his daughter at his side and instinctively reached for her hand, but then quickly retreated, tucking his hands into his pant pockets. In the darkness he had forgotten that Najma was no longer a little girl but a young woman. How much he used to enjoy playing with this daughter of his! As clouds drifted past, revealing a bright, slivered moon, Mr. Jivraj remembered the day he found Najma in the backroom of his *kanga* shop pretending to dance with a bolt of fabric; she had wrapped one end of the fabric around herself like a sari and was holding the bolt out in front of her, stepping this way and that, barely able to keep her balance. The velvety voice of Nat King Cole crooned from the Philips. At first, Mr. Jivraj just stood at the doorway and smiled, but then he marched over and tapped his fingers firmly on the bolt of fabric. "Excuse me, sir, but may I cut in? What? You won't let me dance with the prettiest girl in the whole world? What a crime! Well, all right. I suppose I have no choice." He turned to leave, then snapped back around. "On guard, dacoit!" he yelled, and then executed a flurry of kicks and punches. *"Dashoom!* Take that, bastard. *Dashoom!"* The bolt fell over. Yards and yards of fabric unravelled to expose a beautiful motif of cashews and Swahili proverbs in green and yellow. Mr. Jivraj lifted his daughter, eyes bright, giggling uncontrollably, onto his toes. "I hope I didn't hurt the poor fellow too much, hanh? But then, he didn't stand a bloody chance against me, now did he? After all," he puffed out his chest and wrapped his fingers around his hips, "I am one and only Dilip Kumar, hero-star of the whole world." Najma's head bounced up and down as she looked up at her father.

They danced the entire afternoon, and from then on, he would close the shop for a couple of hours every Saturday afternoon to teach Najma dance routines from all of his favourite films—everything from the "You Excite Me" samba in *Tonight and Every Night* with Rita Hayworth to the *"Pyaar Kiyaa to Dara"* (When You Have Loved, Why Be Afraid?) dance sequence in *Mughal-e-Azam* with Dilip Kumar. Mr. Jivraj asked Najma to keep their dance lessons a secret. He knew his wife would never approve of closing the shop for even one minute. He felt a pang of sadness as he thought about the end of those wonderful afternoons. As he turned and looked at Najma's silhouette, her dress billowing up with the ocean breeze, Yes, he told himself, she will make someone a wonderful wife one day, this beautiful daughter of mine. Mr. Jivraj took a few steps into the ocean and let the receding waves wash away a tangle of seaweed from around his ankles.

Najma removed her shoes, tossing them behind her, and followed her father into the water. She loved the feeling of the ocean and sand between her toes—as if entire worlds could exist on such a small part of her body. She was sure she felt a mermaid's tail tickle her, the smoothness of a polished shell, the kiss of a sailor lost at sea. Carried away with her thoughts, she stepped deeper into the water, prompting Mr. Jivraj to quickly reach forward and cup his hand around her shoulder. "Careful, bheta, not so far!" But it was too late. Najma was already waist-deep in ocean, her dress soaked. "Oh-ho, Najma, your mother's going to be very upset."

Najma's feet sank into the sand. Her father had become such a bloody coward. As far as Najma was concerned, her mother was *always* upset. So what did it matter anyway?

Mr. Jivraj slipped off his jacket and handed it to his daughter as she stepped out of the water. Najma shook her head, but he insisted. When he placed the jacket on her shoulders, he made sure he kept his gaze up from her wet dress. Then he turned away and walked briskly toward the headlights of his car. Najma bent down and splashed more ocean water onto her legs, then turned and followed her father. As she pulled the jacket across her body, she looked ahead at her father's stooping figure. He used to seem so tall, so strong, and Najma was sure that he had somehow shrunk over the years, like a cotton shirt left in hot water too long. Nowadays, he was totally useless. How was it possible, she asked herself, that this was the same man who had taught her how to dance? That he was the same man who had told her endless stories every night, ignoring his wife's insistent screams that it was time for bed. Najma remembered her favourite story—the one from the film *Mughal-e-Azam*—about Prince Saleem and the court dancer Anarkali. King Akbar had promised to crush his son's love affair and bury Anarkali alive, but Prince Saleem rebelled. He was willing to give up his throne and defy his father—all for love.

On the drive back, Mrs. Jivraj hurled insults at both of them, calling Mr. Jivraj a *laloo* and irresponsible, Najma a tomboy and a shameless hussy.

Zarina scolded her too. "You're grown up now, Najma. When are you going to start acting like a young lady?"

Mrs. Jivraj turned back and wagged her finger at Najma. "Exactly! Listen to your sister. Think she would have gotten a boy like Amir Merchant if she was acting like you, *bhadali?*"

Mr. Jivraj didn't say anything.

Najma ignored her sister and her mother. Instead, she stared out at the night sky, which was filled with silent stars, and started her own movie.

FADE IN:

INT. THE POMEGRANATE BALLROOM—EARLY EVENING

NAJMA HAYWORTH, seventeen, simply stunning in a beautiful floor-length red dress and long evening gloves, floats down a staircase leading to the dance floor, her red silk scarf billowing behind her. She takes a long, slow drag from her cigarette, tilts her head back, and blows the smoke out. A crowd of young men in black tails and bow ties gathers at the bottom of the staircase in awe. All heads twist, mouths hang wide open, cigarettes fall to the ground. The crowd parts and on the other side, DILIP KUMAR, debonair in an all-white suit and a silk scarf knotted at his waist and neck, is leaning against the bar. He looks up from his drink in astonishment, crosses the dance floor, and walks straight to her.

DILIP
(Visibly shaken)
Najma, *mera pyar,* I thought you'd
never come. You ... you look simply beautiful in that dress.

Najma looks down at her dress.

NAJMA
Oh, this old thing? It's nothing really.

DILIP
(singing and dancing)
It might be old, my dear,
but I'm so glad you're here.
For if you weren't,
I would have gone mad.
I love your funny face.

NAJMA
Oh, but, darling, don't you know?
That's what I love most about you ...

Najma leans into him.

> NAJMA
> (whispers)
> That you are mad!

Najma reaches for his elbow.

> NAJMA
> Shall we dance, then? They're
> playing our song.

> DILIP
> Where I come from, the man asks
> the girls to dance.

Najma puts out her cigarette, leads him to the dance floor.

> NAJMA
> Well, why not just move *here,* darling?
> Then you won't have to be from *there*
> anymore.

Dilip smiles, shakes his head, and follows her. As they dance, people circle the dance floor; a NEWSPAPER MAN, a large camera around his neck, snaps photographs. *The Tanganyika Standard* whirls to a stop on the screen. The headline reads, "Dar es Salaam's own Bombshell Beauty announces engagement to one and only Hero-Star of the Whole World, Dilip Kumar."

FADE OUT

Mr. Jivraj pulled into the drive and hooted the car horn signalling the *askari* to open the gate to the building. Inside the flat, Mr. Jivraj disappeared into his office. Without being told, Zarina put on a kettle of tea for everyone. Mrs. Jivraj harshly grabbed the bodice of Najma's wet dress and ordered her to change immediately into something dry. *Junglee* girl! Najma pulled herself away from her mother and walked straight to her room, where she flopped onto her bed, landing on her back. She stretched her arm above her, giggling, as she fingered her imagined diamond-studded engagement ring. She pressed her face into a pillow, hoping to contain her laughter, but soon, she started laughing so hard that she started to cry. Her chest heaved up and down as she gasped for air in small desperate breaths.

You Were Never Lovelier

That night, Zarina had the same dream she has had for many years now. It's her ninth birthday and her mother has organized a big party. She and her sister sit in the garden playing with their dolls. Zarina can hear the laughter of all the uncles and aunties inside the house. They are very happy; they have white-painted clown faces, red lipstick, and thick kohl under their eyes. Shokat Uncle is the happiest. He has huge clown shoes and carries armloads of gifts. Zarina tears open her gift. Tattered wrapping paper flies everywhere. Inside is a nesting Russian doll painted in blood red and pea green. Isn't she the most beautiful doll in the whole world? cries Shokat Uncle. Zarina nods eagerly. Pull her head off! yells her mother, her own large head perched on the kitchen windowsill like a flowerpot. Zarina pops the doll open and finds another doll inside, then another, and another, until the very last one. A jellied stone falls out from the smallest doll and onto her lap. It begins to melt, releasing hundreds of maggots, which crawl down her legs, under her dress, over her face, her mouth, down her throat. Zarina screams and throws the doll at Shokat Uncle. She jumps up and down, frantically trying to shake the maggots off. Eh! Is that any way to treat your uncle? Look at how many gifts he has brought for all of us, bellows her mother's head. Say thank you, you ungrateful little girl. No, no, no, Zarina cries. Shokat Uncle bends down and picks her up. Zarina shrinks in his arms. He pinches her between two fingers, brings her to his face. Shokat Uncle inspects her briefly, Zarina's legs dangling under her. You, my dear, were never lovelier, he says, and then turns and winks at Zarina's mother, who is laughing so hard that her head falls off the windowsill and rolls into the muddy flower bed below.

Ladies and Gentlemen, The Pomegranate Ballroom

Amir and Zarina leaned into the mahogany banister that circled the dance floor and watched couples waltzing to the rhythm of Jazzy Joe Fernandez and the Goan All-Stars—all seven of them dressed in black tailcoats and white bow ties, standing on a raised stage decorated with a purple crushed-velvet skirt. Najma sat alone at a nearby table, holding a bottle of Coca-Cola with a red and white straw bobbing in it. Crystal chandeliers imported from Italy hung over the dance floor like miniature glass trees that had been turned upside down and rooted into the ceiling. Bevelled mirrors decorated the wall that faced the dance floor— giving the impression that the ballroom was twice its real size. Amir wrapped his hand around Zarina's waist and pressed himself to her.

Zarina giggled and pulled away, running her hand over her dreamy white dress with its fitted bodice, scooped neck lined with organza flowers, and full skirt layered with organza over netting over crepe—as if it were three dresses, one inside the other inside the other. It flattered Zarina's voluptuous body so that many men could not take their eyes off her, and strangely, many of the women ignored her. Zarina's mother had warned her that this is how women are. They will never like you, bheta. Scared their men will wander with such a beauty around. But if they kept their men happy then what all do they have to worry about, hanh? That is the ultimate question.

It had taken hours and hours for Zarina to get ready for the Grand Opening. Last night, she had carefully laid out her dress on her bed and then placed her glittering gold shoes underneath the trailing hem. After asking her mother, she also chose a new bra and panties set from the many clothes that were purchased to celebrate the engagement. The white lace panties with their side bows and matching bra would, Zarina imagined, make her feel prettier and cleaner. She knew clearly that the Grand Opening was a trial run for the many other evenings Amir would require her to be by his side as he conducted business or entertained his friends and family. She wanted to fulfill her duties flawlessly. Her top priorities were to make a good impression on Amir's business colleagues and, more importantly, she wanted to keep Amir in good spirits. "Will we dance soon?" Zarina asked him, eager to start the evening and showcase her talents to him.

"No point." He tipped his chin toward the dance floor. "Look at how crowded it is."

"How about just a little while?" Zarina said, gently squeezing his elbow. "It is the Grand Opening after all, darling."

"As if I don't know that it's the Grand Opening ..." Amir wrapped his hand firmly around the banister.

"Oh, darling, I don't mind. I was only asking, that's all." Under her dress, Zarina shifted from one leg to the other, ruffling only the innermost layer.

Just then, someone tapped Amir on his shoulder. He turned to see his fast friend from childhood, Hussein Kara—or Topsie, as most people called him, since he was always seen sporting a variety of *topies*—berets, bowlers, top hats, you name it. Amir's and Topsie's families had been next-door neighbours in Kariakoo until the Merchants' business grew from one little ration shop into an empire, after which they moved to a villa in Upanga. Nowadays, Amir and Topsie hardly ever saw each other. "Eh-hey, Mr. Kara. So good of you to come," Amir said as he slapped his friend's arm with one hand and offered the other for a handshake. "Where the hell have you been hiding all evening?"

Topsie reached for Amir's hand. "Hiding, *bana*? Just waiting for my princess to walk through the door, *bas*." He winked.

Amir flicked two fingers against Topsie's hat. "Well, you certainly look like a tip-top prince tonight—so why wait?" He leaned in to Topsie and whispered, "You've got to take the bull by the horns, or should I say cow ..." He then broke out in laughter.

Topsie smiled and shook his head while Zarina joined in on Amir's laughter even though she hadn't heard his comment.

"Well, looks like you've found your princess," Topsie said as he swirled his whisky tumbler; ice cubes clinked against the glass. My God, look at this girl. What a firecracker! Leave it to Amir—lucky bastard. His life was bigger than any Topsie could ever dream of. Amir was a man of the world. He had been to London (and not just once), to Bombay, even Osaka and Tokyo for a textile-buying trip with his father. And each time he returned with stories of all the women—the pearl-white women in

London who had legs longer than a giraffe's, the women in Bombay who were so cheap even a pauper could afford several every night, or the delicate women in Tokyo who were so eager and well-informed that they would do anything you asked, even put their mouths and fingers in unmentionable places. Their mouths? Yes, even their mouths. I'm telling you, first-class whores. Just watching them, removing their clothes, contorting their bodies into the strangest positions, is enough to drive a man mad.

Topsie desperately wished that he had been born into the Merchant family. Life for the Karas had always been a struggle. His father was useless—nothing at all like Mr. Merchant. Mr. Kara had run the family business into the ground, spending most of their money at the casino and on cases of Johnnie Walker. There were even rumours that he was a robber of sorts. A few years ago, when Mr. Kara died in a car accident, Topsie had been relieved. Mrs. Kara wailed at the funeral, beating her chest; Topsie stood firmly next to her, let his hip lean into her, worried that she might fall over. He was clear that as the oldest son it was now his job to be her husband. He resolved to quit school and take care of her and his two little brothers, but Mrs. Kara insisted that he complete his education. "They can take many things away from you, bheta, but no one can take away your education." In the meantime, she would accept Mr. Merchant's generous offer to work in his toy shop. She locked away her wedding jewellery, wore only white, and refused to smile at anyone except the children—but inside, Mrs. Kara hadn't been that happy in years.

"Yes, yes," Amir said proudly as he cupped Zarina's chin in his palm. "This is my princess. Zarina, darling, meet Topsie— pukka friends since childhood."

Zarina nodded hello as Topsie pushed his top hat up with an index finger before taking a long swig of his whisky. Topsie was, in her mind, a buffoon. She had seen him before, at a street corner, wearing that ridiculous white *topie,* singing something from an *angresi* film and offering people dance classes. What kind of man was he? A *shoga,* that's what. She had even seen him grab that old *dosi,* Moti Ma, trying to convince her to take a lesson by swaying his hips this way and that until she thwacked him one with her cane. But that didn't stop him. He removed his top hat and bowed to the *dosima,* who eventually laughed and ruffled his hair. Zarina had been so embarrassed that she quickly crossed the street and walked the other way.

Amir spotted Najma sitting by herself at one of the white-linen-covered tables. She crossed her legs, right over left, left over right, then alternated between snapping the elastic at her waist and adjusting her shoulder strap. He turned to see Zarina calling her sister to them. Oh God, why had Zarina even bothered? Now, they would be stuck with the pathetic girl all night. Doesn't even know how to talk to people properly. Hard to believe that *she* is Zarina's sister.

Najma shot up from her chair and rushed over, bowlegged in her black and white stilettos; she so hoped that Zarina wanted her to dance with Amir.

"What were you doing sitting all by yourself, silly girl?" Zarina plucked a few strands of hair from Najma's face and tucked them behind her ear. I told her that she should have used my V05 hairpsray.

Najma pushed her sister's arm away, then ran her eyes up and down Topsie's body. She had seen this young man in jamatkhana a few times, but she couldn't remember his name. He wasn't exceptionally good-looking, but he wasn't ugly either. He looked quite ordinary except for his white top hat, which towered over him like a column of icing sugar and gave him a magical quality, she thought. She smiled. "Who are you?" she asked, pointing a finger at Topsie.

Zarina quickly tapped Najma's finger down. "Don't be so rude, Najma."

"Oh, this fellow?" Amir asked. "This is Topsie Kara, number one dancer in the whole of Dar es Salaam. No, no, the whole of Tanganyika. I say maybe even all of Africa. What do *you* say, Topsie?" Amir laughed as he winked at his friend. Once, when they were still neighbours, Amir and Topsie slipped onto the grounds of the British Gymkhana Club to watch the Europeans dancing—their shadows illuminated in the soft yellow glow of the window screens. "Bastards!" Amir shook his head. "Just worried that their women will be overwhelmed with our excellent physiques and our mind-boggling abilities on the dance floor. Not to mention our capacity off the dance floor, *bana.*" "Exactly!" Topsie echoed as they both doubled over in laughter. "Correction, correction," Amir said, standing up straight and jesting his thumbs to his chest. "I meant *my* mind-boggling abilities." He took two steps back, swayed his hips and shoulders, and pretended to dance the rumba. *"Ur-ruh-ruh!"* Topsie countered, his palms turned to the sky. "You call that dancing, *bana*? Please stop it before I vomit. It's a good thing no one can see us here," Topsie lightly cuffed Amir's chin, "because you, sir, are an embarrassment to all good men. If you want to dance, Merchant, let me show you a thing or two." Topsie removed his hat, bowed, and then began a series of demonstrations using the palm tree as his partner—the fox trot, samba, Viennese waltz. Amir watched impatiently, his hands on his hips, until he couldn't bear it anymore. If there was one thing he couldn't stand, it was a show-off! "Stop it now," Amir ordered, and grabbed Topsie's arm. "I've seen more than enough, thank you very much." But Topsie pulled away and playfully ducked behind a tree, taunting Amir to catch him. "Stop acting so childish," Amir said, lunging forward. He caught the tail of Topsie's shirt and yanked him forward before jumping onto his back and coiling his legs around Topsie like a snake. "Such a featherweight you are," Topsie teased, and continued dancing. Frustrated, Amir pushed himself off and then whipped Topsie around to him, shaking him by his shoulders. "Are you deaf or what? I said stop dancing!" Amir's words bellowed out in the same firm tone his father used when he reprimanded Amir for any errors in bookkeeping. "Who the hell do you think you are? The Fred Astaire of Dar? Let me tell you a thing or two, my friend. You might be better in all this dancing-shmancing business, but in things that really count, we all know that I am king." Soon after, the Merchants bought the villa in Upanga.

Amir slipped his arms around Topsie and Najma. "Go on now. Show the girl your fancy steps, why don't you?" He pursed his lips and pushed the couple forward. "You are, after all, the Fred Astaire of Dar, aren't you?" *Let's see how good he is with a baboon for a partner.*

Topsie felt his face stiffen; he shot Amir a dirty look. *Of all the girls in Dar, why her?* Najma stepped toward Topsie, still smiling broadly.

"I don't know if this is such a good idea," Zarina said, swinging her gold-sequined purse behind her. "Pappa won't like it one bit if he finds out Najma's been dancing." *What was wrong with Najma? Didn't she know that this Topsie fellow was a complete idiot?*

"Why does Pappa have to find anything out?" Najma asked as she slipped her hand into the crook of Topsie's arm.

"Exactly." Amir pressed his fingers into Topsie's shoulder and pushed him forward. "Go on now. No need to feel shy, Topsie. Let's see the master at work." Amir took Zarina's hand in his and pulled her to the railing overlooking the dance floor. He couldn't wait to watch the spectacle.

"Don't listen to Amir, he's a first-class exaggerator," Topsie said to Najma. "I'm really not that good."

"Oh, I'm not that good either," Najma said.

"Perfect, we're made for each other, then." Topsie removed his hat and bowed. "After you, madam."

Najma eyes brightened. The words *made for each other* played over and over in her mind and she wanted to savour them as she would a sweetmeat.

Najma's head came to Topsie's neck, and she could smell the faint scent of his cologne and the familiar smell of cigarette smoke. Suddenly, she became nervous, realizing that she'd never been this close to a man's body. She was no longer sure if she would be able to dance in her heels. But then Topsie pressed his hand on the concavity of her back, and Najma felt free of the constraints of gravity and floated effortlessly in his arms.

It had always been difficult to dance with other girls, so Topsie was genuinely surprised at how easily he moved with Najma—as if they were cut from the same cloth. He squeezed her hand in his and when he felt the pulse of her fingertips on his skin, he felt compelled to pull her closer. Shocked by his action, he quickly retreated. Najma smiled and brought him back to her. Topsie spread his palm on the small of her back and whispered, "And you said you couldn't dance? You're better than Ginger Rogers and Madhubala put together."

Najma leaned back. "Ginger Rogers? Don't be mad. You mean Rita, don't you? Rita Hayworth."

Topsie winked, pulling her back to him. He let his lips graze the top of her ear. "Of course, my mistake. The only difference is that you're more beautiful."

A frisson of pleasure ran through Najma's body, making her open like the plush velvet curtains at the Empire Theatre. For the first time, Najma felt as if there was no difference between the outside and the inside of her—she felt beautiful and she was beautiful. She had never experienced such euphoria before, and knew instantly what it all meant. Her hero-prince had finally arrived.

To Amir's surprise, Topsie and Najma danced together as if they belonged to air, gliding together with such ease that they looked as if they were one. But what shocked Amir was Najma. He couldn't take his eyes off her. There was something about the way she moved her body, the way her hips swayed freely under her silk dress. Strangely, he wanted to take her in his arms and make her his. This image evoked such an intense pleasure in Amir that for a brief moment he imagined lying on her, his body swallowed by hers. But only seconds later, he was repulsed by the thought. *What the hell is wrong with me? Good God, have I had that much to drink that I can't see who this girl really is? A whore, a filthy whore.* He glanced at Zarina, who was still at his side. *Now, there's a woman. A real beauty.* He quickly brushed off his lapel and buttoned his jacket, pulling it down a little before he took Zarina's hand in his. "Come, darling, let me introduce you to my friends."

It was getting late—when would they ever dance? Zarina wondered. She wanted to say something, but instead she nodded and followed Amir as he led her through the crowd. Many people stopped them. They were eager to congratulate Amir on the opening of the Ballroom *(wa-wa!)* and on his recent engagement to Zarina *(wa-wa!)*. A match made in heaven, one man said. Zarina smiled, making sure she laughed at all the men's jokes and blushed at their compliments. She held on to Amir, tightening her grip around his arm when they were introduced to the men's fiancées or wives. They continued until they reached the back, where they stopped at the circular mahogany bar. Amir leaned over the counter and ordered a whisky, neat, for himself and a Fanta for Zarina. The men sitting at the bar swivelled their stools and openly surveyed Zarina, their eyes shifting up and down her body. One of the men pulled Amir in and whispered, "What a bombshell, *bana*." Amir gave him a thumbs-up and then ordered a round of Johnnie Walker for all the men, who responded with loud applause.

As Amir handed Zarina her drink, he told her that he wanted to talk to the men about business. One man chuckled. "Wait for me at the table," Amir instructed.

"All right, darling. Nice to meet all of you," Zarina said, and turned to leave.

As Zarina walked away, all the men's heads turned, following her retreat like the needle of a compass.

Zarina returned to their table where she sat, staring blankly into the crowded dance floor—as if she were a pin-up girl tacked to the chair. She couldn't believe it was almost the end of the night and they still hadn't danced. Why wouldn't Amir dance with her? She quickly retrieved a pocket mirror from her purse, checked her hair, and then reapplied her ruby red lipstick. Oh God, had she done something wrong, something to put him off? This question spun in her like a reel of film on a movie projector, until her eyes caught Najma. Suddenly, Zarina was overwhelmed with worry: Look at the way she's dancing with Topsie. Did Najma want to jeopardize their family's reputation—dancing with her body pasted to such a low-class fool—especially with the wedding only weeks away? Zarina put down her Fanta with such strength that the orange liquid fizzed to the top of the bottle. She weaved through the crowd, pushing several couples out of her way. They turned in anger but softened as soon as they saw it was Zarina.

Zarina pulled her sister to the side. "Come on, we're leaving," she whispered sharply.

"Oh, Zarina, can't we stay just little longer? Please."

"Stop acting like a *rakhroo!*" Zarina grabbed Najma's elbow. "Everyone is looking at you." She kept a firm grip on Najma's arm and rushed her off the dance floor. "This is for your own good, Najma. You better stay away from that hoodlum."

"But we weren't doing anything."

"You don't understand how boys are." Zarina squeezed Najma's arm. "Besides, don't you know who he is? His father was the biggest dacoit in all of Tanganyika. And his mother? Useless.

Totally useless. Works at Amir's toy shop. They're paupers, Najma. Imagine a life with people like them."

Topsie trailed behind the sisters and when he reached them, tapped Zarina on her shoulder. "One sec, please."

Zarina turned around, shrinking back when she saw Topsie.

"Please, I'm so very sorry," Topsie said, removing his hat. "If I offended you in some way, please forgive me. My intentions are honourable."

Of course they are, Zarina thought. He probably wants to marry into our family now that he's heard about *my* engagement to Amir.

Najma released herself from her sister's grip. "He didn't do anything, Zarina."

"Didn't do anything? Dancing together as if you're a married couple? If Mummy and Pappa hear, they'll kill you. Imagine what people would say! Come on, let's go. Pappa gave us strict orders to be home by midnight. And you," she said, scowling at Topsie. "Stay away from my sister, understand? And don't you think for even one second that Amir won't hear about this." As Zarina led Najma away, Najma untied the scarf around her neck, turned back to Topsie, smiling, and let it fall to the ground.

From Here to Eternity

Soon after, Topsie confessed his love for Najma to Amir and asked him to deliver a note to her wrapped in her scarf.

"Are you mad, Topsie? Don't you have eyes? Of all the girls in Dar, why her?" He put his arm around Topsie. "I know she's going to be my sister-in-law, *bana,* but come on, she's pathetic, truly pathetic." Topsie insisted, and Amir continued to resist, giving him all sorts of reasons why he shouldn't. "Aye, imagine seeing her face every morning—in full daylight, *bana.*" Topsie didn't give up and offered counter-arguments. "To me, she is the most beautiful woman in the world. I can't stop thinking of her. I know this is love. This is love."

Amir just laughed and mocked him, frustrating Topsie further, until he had a realization. "Oh, I see. Zarina is making you spoil my plans. Got you under her thumb, hanh?"

"Don't be ridiculous, *bana.*"

"I don't blame you—I'd do anything Najma asked me to do too. But I beg you, please take this one note to her. I just have to see her alone once, that's all."

"Bloody hell!" Amir snatched the knotted scarf and shoved it in his pocket. "You'll regret it, Topsie. I'm telling you. You can do so much better than that girl. Look at the girl I've got."

As Amir turned to leave, Topsie begged him not to say anything to Zarina. "Otherwise, she'll spoil everything."

What a bloody idiot! Amir thought when he read the note. No wonder Topsie's family never amounted to much. How could he possibly have fallen for Najma? But then he laughed to himself. Wait 'til Topsie gets her alone and sees the *bhadali* properly, then it will be completely different story. Amir delivered the note, wrapped in Najma's scarf, at another family dinner.

When Najma read the note, she imagined herself running toward Topsie in a tall field of grass, monsoon rains pouring down on them, her tight *langa* patterned with mirrors soaked, and *"Ek Ladki Ko Dekha"* from *1942 Love Story* booming in the background.

Rita, *mera pyar,*

Please meet me tomorrow night outside the Ballroom after jamatkhana. I can't bear another night of not seeing you! (A driver will be waiting outside your flat, back entrance.)

Call me mad, but I love your funny, funny face.

Forever yours,

Fred

Beauty and the Beasts

Zarina dreamt that she was a movie star. Curtains rise at the Empire Theatre. The title across the screen reads BOMBSHELL BEAUTY STARRING ZARINA JIVRAJ. Men in the audience hoot and holler, even throw popcorn at the screen. The camera cuts to Zarina walking down a red carpet; men whistle and clap. But soon, the whistles become growls, and when Zarina turns to the men, she sees that they have heads of wolves. Run, her sleeping self tells Zarina in the dream. Run! The pack of men chases her and just as they lunge at her, their paws suspended in mid-air, Zarina bursts out of the movie and lands on the stage of the Empire Theatre, leaving a hole the shape of her body on the screen. She is covered with blood and debris. The audience boos. Mothers shield their children's eyes. Some quickly lead their families away. Men pound their fists on their armrests. One man stands up, a rock the size of a cricket ball in his hand. The audience roars with applause and screams of excitement. *Go, go, go!* they chant and stamp their feet when the man winds his arm like a bowler at a cricket match.

Zarina bolted up in her bed. Her eyes were filled with tears and her floral cotton nightie was soaked with perspiration. "What is wrong with me? Please, God, help me," she said. But she knows he's not listening. She thought about how terrifyingly lonely she was even with her parents in the room next door, her little sister in the bed beside hers. In this moment, Zarina wanted to crawl into bed with Najma, like she used to when they were younger, and feel the warmth of her sister's body beside her. She slipped out of her bed and reached to wake Najma, but she was not there. First, Zarina checked the bathroom, then the entire flat. My God, where was she? Had some dacoit crawled into their room and abducted her sister? Zarina shook with horror and ran to her parents' room. She was about to open their door when a thought occurred to her: She's with that hoodlum! She searched Najma's things and found the love letter tucked under her mattress. Oh my God, Najma. What have you done?

Zarina rushed quietly to the front door, a flashlight in one hand and a shilling note in the other. She struck the necessary deal with the *askari*. Outside the ballroom, Zarina asked the *askari* to drop her off and then wait a few streets over. She checked the front door of the ballroom. Locked. She pressed her face to the window. Nothing. It was pitch dark. She was scared to continue, but knew she had to. Her sister was in grave danger. She turned on the flashlight and pointed it down the alley like a gun from a holster. The light caught a row of crates neatly stacked against the wall. She tentatively made her way toward the back of the building, and was about to turn the corner when she noticed a dim light in the window above. She stepped up on a crate and peered in.

I Spy

Amir parked his car across from the Ballroom and waited. He was not sure why, but he felt a perverse pleasure in spying on Najma—that whore. Eventually, he saw two figures, one holding a long flashlight, as they walked quickly down an alleyway toward the back of the ballroom. Amir stepped out of his car and surveyed the street. The streets were, thankfully, empty with the exception of a few beggars. "Spare some change?" a man spread on a tattered gunny sack asked. Amir reached into his pocket and tossed a coin at him. "*Waweza kuangalia vitu gari, bana?* Watch the car?" The beggar asked for more if he was going to be a watchman. Amir was about to refuse, but he didn't want to create a ruckus at his hour. He dug into his pocket and gave the old man a few more coins before he crossed the street to the building; a large sign on the top read, MERCHANT ENTERPRISES PRESENTS THE POMEGRANATE BALLROOM.

Amir walked to the side of the building, where he noticed several fallen crates. *Mbafu* servants. Never do any job to satisfaction! As he picked up the crates and placed them neatly against the wall, he saw a cone of light flit like a firefly from window to window and then settle into a frame near the front. He quickly squatted and waited for a few seconds before crawling to the window on all fours. Then he inched up, placing his fingertips on the filthy window ledge, and peered in. Inside, Topsie and Najma danced to a silent orchestra. How the hell had he managed to get in? That bloody dacoit—must have learned some tricks from his thieving father. Amir could barely see them; the flashlight created only dim shadows on the wall behind them. It was like watching a silent film. How boring! A few minutes later, Amir became weary—he was wasting his time. But then he saw Najma's silhouette bend to pick up the flashlight from the floor. Look at that! Round and thick like a pig! Amir shook his head in amusement. Is Topsie completely out of his mind? I suppose a pig in the dark is better than a pig in broad daylight. Amir laughed out loudly, fumbling on some crates.

Topsie turned toward the window. Amir dropped down. A few seconds later, he lifted his head, his eyes just above the base of the window, and watched the cone of light move from window to window, this time from the middle of the ballroom to the back. *Trying to keep your liaisons with that girl a secret, hanh, Topsieji? Who can blame him really? He'd be the laughingstock of Dar!*

Excited at the idea of a pursuit, Amir followed along the side of the building until the light disappeared and there was nothing but darkness and silence. At the back of the building, he picked up another crate and pushed it to the wall. Through the barred window, he could see Najma fumbling at her neck. She untied her scarf and draped it on the flashlight, which had been placed on a chair like a candle. Now he could only see when Najma and Topsie moved closer to the flashlight. It was like watching a damaged film—only flashes were illuminated. *Bloody hell! What does she think—this is romantic? Pathetic. Romantic in a shoddy backroom? Try the London Savoy, maybe. What a first-class whore, going to the backroom with a man she hardly knows.* Amir leaned in, his chin on the window ledge, his hands wrapped around the bars. As he watched, Amir now began to imagine a sweater coming off a shoulder, the muscles of a neck released backward, wet lips on a collarbone, the plumpness of a breast, the flesh of a thigh jiggling against tweed, fingers stumbling with a buckle, a head full of dark unruly hair lowering. He pressed his face to the bars. Amir couldn't help himself. He let his left hand drop off the bar, his fingertips covered with grime. He unzipped his pants and reached inside.

ZARINA PUSHED HERSELF up on her tiptoes, steadying herself on the windowsill, but she still could not see anything. She wasn't high enough. She stepped down, picked up a crate, and squared it on top of the one she had been standing on. She then glanced both ways before pulling her dress up to free her knees. Yes, much better, she thought as she climbed up and then cupped her hands to the window. Even still, Zarina could see only fragments of a couple inside, but she could hear the muffled rhythm of feet, like hooves on fields of wet grass. They were dancing! Zarina's immediate impulse was to bang a fist to the glass and make her sister stop, but instead she leaned in, eager first to make out their faces, confirm that it was them.

As Zarina waited patiently to catch a glimpse of her sister, she found herself tapping her toe to the crate, mimicking and amplifying the rhythms inside the ballroom. Soon, she started to sway her hips to match her feet. The swaying, like a trance, transported Zarina, so that the alley was turned into a ballroom and now it was *her* dancing. She imagined herself striding onto the dance floor, where she easily commanded the steps of even the most difficult routines—the Viennese waltz, the fox trot, the rumba. During one sequence, when her partner swung her away with one quick snap of his wrist, Zarina, like a sleepwalker, jumped off the stacked crates. *Thump!* She landed squarely on both feet, so that she felt as if her body had been snapped into place. Her breath was unencumbered, reaching, it seemed, each corner of her body for the very first time. She was light and free. The flashlight caught Zarina's foot, illuminating it. She pointed the beam forward, coyly stepping into it and then following it down the alley like a dancer being called onto a stage.

AMIR PRACTICALLY FELL OFF the crate when he turned, in shock, toward the flashlight being pointed at him. He quickly pressed himself to the wall, his hands fumbling as he tucked himself back into his pants.

Zarina gasped with terror when she saw a man standing in the back alley. It took her a few seconds to realize that this was no beggar, no shadowy mugger. This was her fiancé! She was now overcome with relief and excitement. "Darling!" she squealed, still in a partial trance. It was as if Amir had followed her stage directions and appeared, like a wish, in front of her. Zarina rushed to him, but when she reached him, she suddenly became nervous, and no longer knew what to do.

Amir looked down at the figure in front of him and in the darkness, all he could see was the top of her head—as if it was suspended in mid-air, severed from the body. What in God's name was she doing here? He stepped down from the crate, ready to reprimand her, but then his eyes met hers and he couldn't help but be enthralled by her. Look at her! She is so beautiful. His body was still aching with pleasure and he felt compelled to take her in his arms.

Zarina was excited by Amir's touch, thrilled to be in his arms—finally! She nudged him forward. "Let's dance!" she blurted out.

Without thinking, Amir accepted. He pulled her in to him and then swung her away. Zarina leaned back and spun around him, like a planet to the sun, his presence warming her, making her feel alive. She flung her head back and watched the stars spinning above her as if they were rearranging themselves, creating new constellations.

Amir pulled her close again, and in her excitement, Zarina pressed herself to him. He now felt his hardness against her and was suddenly embarrassed. What is wrong with her? My God, this was his future wife in his arms! He was filled with anger and disgust. In that moment, he wanted to reach down, pick up the flashlight, and smash it into her head. Instead he pushed her off him. Zarina flew back and hit the ground.

She gasped for air, her mind still in a daze. When she looked up and saw her fiancé glaring at her, she now felt ashamed. She quickly cast her eyes down.

Amir was about to rush away, but then his heart suddenly softened as he looked at Zarina sitting on the ground, helpless. He now felt a great need to take care of her, to protect her as a guard dog would a property. He bent down and cupped his hand to her elbow. "Come," he whispered as he tried to lift her, but she was so heavy, like a rag doll filled with stones, that he struggled.

Zarina tried to steady herself between the arms of the man she would spend the rest of her life with, but she could barely stand up, until her eyes caught the soft glow of light inside the ballroom and then, suddenly, she found her strength as a hot ember of rage and envy began to flicker inside of her.

Open House

Rubina Mawji pulls her silver Nissan Maxima in front of 314 Sunset Vista Drive, where she is conducting an Open House between 2 and 4 P.M. The house is located in Signal Hill, one of Calgary's newer areas, and offers spectacular views of the city as well as the Rockies. The house itself has excellent curb appeal—an important feature when selling a house. It is landscaped beautifully and has a wraparound patio. Other features of the house include: three bedrooms, two and a half baths, a custom kitchen with granite countertops, new appliances including a gas barbeque built into the deck, and a fire pit in the back garden. It is also in excellent condition, and only seven years old.

It should be easy to sell, but Rubina—or Ruby as most people call her—has had some trouble. This is the third weekend in a row that she has had to conduct an Open House here—a rarity for Ruby, who is often able to sell a house well above the asking price, in one week flat. It's no wonder that she is touted at Stampede Realty as the fastest gun in the West. Before Ruby joined the company, it took an average of thirty days to sell a house. Thanks to her, the company average has dropped to twenty-one days.

Ruby knows, as every realtor knows, the longer a house sits on the market, the harder it is to sell. Buyers grow more fearful with each passing day, wondering why no one has bought it yet. Speed is essential. It's what differentiates good agents from top agents like Ruby. Her face, with its broad reassuring smile, appears on bus shelters and benches across Calgary. Perched on her head, a golden crown with a dazzling red ruby. Her slogan: 24-Karat Success Guaranteed! In fact, Ruby is so confident of her abilities that she offers to buy your house herself if she can't sell it.

Even the men at Stampede Reality marvel at Ruby's abilities, and if she were younger, for Ruby is now forty-two, then many of them might even make lewd comments about her at the pub or else imagine how her prowess might translate to the bedroom. Instead, they casually flirt with her, telling her what a crying shame it is that she's already married. Not that any one of them would really want to be her husband. The poor guy! We all know who wears the pants in that family, hey? Betcha that woman's a ball-buster, hey?

The current owners of 314 Sunset Vista, Lynda and Lance Nickel, have already purchased another house and are eager for Ruby to sell this house quickly. They do not want to carry two mortgages for much longer. Ruby advised them to wait before purchasing another home, or at minimum, to purchase the other house—which she had helped them find—on the condition that this one would sell. But the Nickels refused. They did not want to live here anymore. Lynda had miscarried three times. All tests confirmed that there was nothing wrong with her, and now, the Nickels are convinced that the source of the problem was the electricity tower located behind their house, only a few metres from their property line.

Recently, there has been extensive media attention on the dangers of electricity towers. Beyond being an eyesore and blocking the view, research indicates electromagnetic fields could pose health threats, might even lead to infertility or cancer. Some experts say that the research is inconclusive and that the media, as always, is generating unnecessary fear. But several environmental advocacy groups disagree. One group is lobbying to replace the towers with underground wiring or else relocate them at a safer distance; yet another is demanding the wholesale removal of the towers, and suggesting the city adopt alternative sources of energy, such as wind power. This group has also organized protests, some of which have included home owners wrapping police tape around the perimeter of their houses or placing signs in their windows that read, BEWARE: ELECTRICAL TOWERS IN AREA!

At previous Open Houses, Ruby tried to reassure potential buyers that the house was safe by providing them with a report prepared by Dwayne Olson, a house inspector that Ruby has employed on numerous occasions. Using a Gauss meter, Dwayne certified that the electromagnetic field emitted from the electricity towers was, in his expert opinion, nothing to worry about. "Microwaves and computers emit far more when all combined!" Ruby said to wary buyers. But this tactic did not seem to quell their fears, so Ruby decided more had to be done. She contracted Dwayne to prepare a short video that she could play during the Open House—one that demonstrates his findings. "People need to see what you're talking about. It's the only way they'll understand that there's nothing to be scared of. I want them to have the facts. Ignorance breeds fear, you know," Ruby said to Dwayne.

"Man, Ruby. You think of it all, don't ya? Those poor people won't know what's hit them," Dwayne said, shaking his head and laughing.

Ruby didn't say anything—Dwayne wouldn't understand. How could he? He was a house inspector, someone whose job it was to point out problems, not solve them as she had to. Ruby takes great pride in her work and feels tremendous satisfaction in solving a problem for a client—it is like fitting all the pieces of a puzzle together. In fact this is how she built her business, her reputation as an agent who'd go the extra mile, do whatever it takes to make the sale. Her mind, like a calculator, works out various combinations and permutations until she is able to find the right solution for her client. So that if Ruby is presented with a problem such as the bathroom being too small, she contracts a designer to help draw up plans for how the house could accommodate a larger bathroom, or if there is rot in the foundation, then she solicits, at her own cost, a second opinion, and if the results are the same, then she provides quotes of how to get rid of it. She has struck deals with many builders and subcontractors in the city to help in the process. As Ruby has always said, with enough ingenuity, you can solve anything.

Yet when Ruby discovered earlier this week that her husband Firoz was having an affair, she did not do anything about it, did not try to solve this problem. She didn't ask him for any details, didn't probe as she might a customer for the whats and whys, eager to respond with her expert skills in Objection Handling. There was no point. After all, this has been an ongoing problem for years now. Firoz, it seems, is able to duplicate his lovers in much the same way he might copy a document at one of his stores, Encore Printing. Ruby often wonders what these other women see in him. But what does it matter? It only makes her life easier. At least he's out of my hair!

Ruby turns off the ignition and then takes a sip of her coffee before tossing the paper cup into a small plastic garbage can. It lands on a pile of crumpled-up Wendy's serviettes, Flake chocolate bar wrappers, and Diet Coke cans. Ruby is usually diligent about taking care of herself—eating well, working out for an hour each morning on the StairMaster or else to a Jane Fonda video, but on weekends, she often eats out—a consequence of being on the go, always rushing from one Open House to another. She enjoys the speed of her life—even if there are some days that she tires. It makes her feel like she's maximizing each day, not wasting even one minute.

Ruby flings open her car door and steps out, her arms filled with files and a small box. She turns and slams the door closed with her foot—another good reason not to drive an expensive car. You don't have to worry about keeping it in immaculate condition. She doesn't care that the bumper is dented, and is now showing signs of rust, or that the passenger side door has several dings. Not that Ruby can't afford a nicer car—like a BMW or a Mercedes, the kind of car many other agents of her calibre seem to drive—but she feels it's important not to show off. Clients don't want to see how you spend their money. Besides, she prefers putting her money toward more practical things, like her son Alim's education. She hopes that one day he will go to an Ivy League school in the States, maybe even Harvard like the Imam.

Next door, a group of girls is busy chalking the sidewalk. One girl is lying down, her arms and legs spread out, while another girl squats next to her, tracing her body. "Looks like fun, ladies," Ruby says cheerfully. She loves children. When they first married, Ruby and Firoz joked that they would have enough children to populate a small town. They even had a list tacked to the fridge of possible names. It started with Alim/Alyshah and ended with Zia/Zarah.

Ruby heads up the walkway to the house, her heels clicking against the cement. A sign in the centre of the lawn reads, PESTI-CIDE FREE. She retrieves a key from the lock box wrapped around the doorknob, and unlocks the front door.

The house was empty at previous Open Houses—the Nickels had already moved their furniture to their new house—yet another factor, Ruby is certain, that has made it hard to sell. People need to visualize what their lives would be like in a house before they can consider buying it. Without furniture or any belongings, that's very difficult, if not impossible for most people. Today, Ruby has made arrangements with a local designer to stage the house. It is now filled with beautiful furniture, artwork, books, even family portraits—of whom, Ruby does not know.

Selling a house is like hosting a dinner party, Ruby has always thought. Preparation is the key. You have to think through every single detail, right down to the colour of the napkins and the music you'll play, so that when your guests arrive you don't have to worry about a thing. You can put all your energy into enter-taining—which is really the best part, isn't it? The only difference is that at an Open House, you don't have to cook or clean! And you get to go home at the end of the evening. This is not your house.

There is no such thing as luck, Ruby often tells the many new agents who come to her clamouring for advice. Luck is when Preparation meets Opportunity. She doesn't reveal her sources to the men, but she candidly tells the women that these are Oprah's words, not hers. Ruby tapes the show and watches it each week-night after she comes home from jamatkhana.

Ruby walks through the house making sure everything is in order. It's spotless, and there are fresh-cut flowers in almost every room. But Ruby still straightens pillows and adds her own touches. She lights a candle with the scent Fresh Grass and slides open several windows, running a paper towel along the sills. When she spots a partially decomposed wasp between the panes of a window, she plucks it out with the paper towel and then tosses it into a garbage can.

Ruby turns on her laptop and waits for it to boot up. Until recently, this laptop had been Alim's, but he wanted a new one, one that was more powerful.

"Good God, Ruby, it's the cost of a small car," Ruby's younger sister, Shelina, said when she heard, rolling her eyes. Shelina has two children, a boy and a girl, and often accuses Ruby of spoiling Alim. Once, when they'd gone to Earl's for coffee and dessert after Panje Bhenu majlis, a special ceremony for women only, she wagged her fork at Ruby and said, half laughing, "Just make sure my kids don't get wind of what his allowance is, hmm? They'll have my head."

Ruby clucked her tongue, pushing her fork into her cheese-cake. "Come on, Shel. You know what a good kid he is. He deserves it." Not only was Alim at the top of his class at Strathcona–Tweedsmuir, the best private school in Calgary, but he also ranked third in the city's tennis tournament last year—

after which Ruby and Firoz took him, on her suggestion, to the U.S. Open for their sixteenth wedding anniversary. Alim also volunteers on Saturdays at Headquarters Jamatkhana, teaching grade-one Bait-ul Ilm classes. It's essential to give back, Ruby has always said to him. She herself is heavily involved in various voluntary committees like the Resettlement Committee, which helps newly arrived Afghani Ismailis settle in and become self-sufficient quickly—Canadian taxpayers, understandably, do not want yet another drain on their hard-earned money. Ruby is also the Chairperson of the Economic Planning Board—a post that takes much of her time so that she often has to survive on as little as four hours' sleep. But it was all well worth it. Under her leadership, she had initiated a campaign on the importance of buying a home as well as comprehensive financial planning courses for women. Many speculate that with all her successes she might one day be the first woman appointed Council President.

"And so what if I spoil him a little?" Ruby asked her sister, trying to hide her frustration. Isn't that what she has worked so hard for all these years, to build a life in which she could raise Alim properly? How different am I from any other mother? What mother wants to see her child suffer? Ruby refuses to let her son go without, or to be wrought with worry about money, as she had been when she was growing up.

When Ruby was twelve and Shelina seven, their parents sent them to study at the Forrest Hill Girls Boarding School in

London. Tanzania was becoming increasingly unstable and Ruby's parents, like so many others, worried for their children's safety. Julius Nyerere had called for all non-owner occupied buildings and homes to be nationalized, but Ruby's father had not wanted to leave the country just yet. Luckily, the new law did not affect Ruby's family. They owned a sugar-cane farm and processing plant in Magugu, near Arusha, and business was still good. But who knew when it might be taken away? Might as well make as much money as we can now.

Many other Ismaili girls lived at the boarding school, but Ruby's parents wanted a home environment for their daughters, one in which they would not come under any outside influences. They made arrangements for Ruby and Shelina to stay with their mother's younger sister, Gulshan, and her husband, Pyarali. Gulshan had recently given birth to her first son, and welcomed the idea of having extra help around the house. Ruby and Shelina arrived in England in the winter of 1970. They saw their parents for two weeks each year, but it would take nine years before they were reunited.

Gulshan Aunty was kind to Ruby and Shelina, and made every effort to make them feel at home, miss their own parents less. But Pyarali Uncle had not wanted them there and treated them as if they were a burden, hinting that they should never take second helpings, or banging on the bathroom door during their baths: "Don't use all the bloody hot water!" It did not take long for Ruby to start plotting a way out. She started saving her lunch stipend, storing it in a jar under her bed. She walked with her head down, forever searching for coins others may have dropped. But then Gulshan Aunty found the jar and, possibly without thinking, mentioned it to Pyarali Uncle. He was certain that they'd been stealing from him. Ruby protested and told him that it was her lunch money. "The way you eat, you expect me to believe that?" He took both girls to the back garden. "I will not tolerate thieves in this house." Ruby kicked and screamed. "Please, do what you want to me, but Shelina didn't do anything!" "One bad apple spoils the barrel," he said, before he pulled Shelina into the shed, slamming the door behind him. Inside, he held her wrist above her head, as he would later hold Ruby's, and burned her index and middle finger with a cigarette lighter. Ruby tried to open the door, pushing and pulling the latch, banging her fists to the wall, but it remained closed. Ruby fell to her knees, pressing her hands over her ears, but she could still hear her sister screaming.

That night, Ruby packed their things and they took the tube to Heathrow, where they slept in the departures lounge. Over the next few weeks, she organized to find a job and moved into a small flat in Ilford with three other Ismaili girls, also students at Forrest Hill. Ruby was fifteen, Shelina ten. They would live on their own, Ruby working a part-time job for years—first as a cashier at Sainsbury's and later in the food hall at Harrods—until, four years later, her parents asked them to return to Arusha. To this day, Ruby's mother and Gulshan Aunty don't speak.

That day at Earl's, Ruby took the last bite of her cheesecake, still keen on making her point clear to her sister. "You know I make Alim work for it."

"Work for it? Ha! You call picking up your socks working for it? I wish I had you as a boss." Shelina is a dental hygienist, but she doesn't like the work and she certainly doesn't like the dentist she works for. She complains about her boss incessantly. She only has two weeks' holiday and her breaks are strictly monitored. Dr. Dalton also refuses to let her take time off when her children are sick. To make things worse, Shelina's husband hardly helps around the house, or with the children, so that Shelina often feels overwhelmed.

Ruby has tried to encourage her sister to find another job, or, if not that, to at least brainstorm possible solutions to her problems. "Why not get a maid every couple of weeks?" she asked, to which Shelina responded, "Not everyone can afford the lifestyle of the rich and famous, Ruby." And if Ruby tried to give her tips on improving her efficiency, Shelina often dismissed her or said something sarcastic, "We're not all Superwoman, you know."

Ruby sometimes feels like shaking her sister by the shoulders. You need to take responsibility for your life! What's the use in blaming others? Complaining all day long. It'll only drain you— all this negative energy. With the right attitude, you'll be amazed at what you can accomplish. "Each time you overcome you become stronger and stronger, so that one day you wake up and realize you're powerful," Oprah had once explained to a distressed guest. "I'm telling you, people, I've said it once and I'll say it a thousand times: Power equals Strength over Time." Absolutely true! Ruby thought. Look at me, Ruby wants to say to Shelina. No doubt, I've had my share of ups and downs. But that's what's made me who I am today. A tough-minded, independent woman. If anything, Ruby's hardships have only made her appreciate her life even more. In fact, she feels so blessed that in her wallet she carries a list of all the reasons she should be thankful. At the top of Ruby's list, Alim. He is her *jaan,* her life really, and there isn't anything she wouldn't do for him.

These days, Ruby just listens to her sister without offering any advice, but more often than not, she finds her mind wandering, thinking of the many items on her schedule.

The laptop screen lights up and fills with a picture of the Imam in a white polo shirt, next to an Arabian horse. The screen is slightly damaged in one spot, creating a void in the horse's right eye, as if the pupil has been erased. Ruby double-clicks on *My Music,* selecting a folder named *Relaxing Classical,* which contains tracks that Alim has downloaded for her from the Internet. Alim also showed her how to use the laptop, patiently giving her tutorials after their weekly date when they prepare dinner together from one of their many cookbooks. Their current favourite: Jamie Oliver's new book, *Pukka Tukka.* Alim cleaned the laptop of all viruses and defragmented the hard-drive (terms he taught her) before he loaded it with extra software, including a faster Internet browser. Ha! Ruby laughs as she turns up the speaker volume. Imagine how much time I would have saved if the Internet existed a few years ago. It would have been so much easier to track Firoz's activities. She could have requested a copy of his Visa bill online instead of having to steam open envelopes. She could have purchased surveillance equipment on eBay instead of wasting her time trailing him after work. She could even have googled his latest lover. Thank God those days are long gone!

Each time Ruby suspected an affair she would meticulously gather evidence and then present it to Firoz—the first few times in a fit of anger, and then later, in an effort to make him stop. She refused to let their marriage end without a fight. It was as if Firoz was sinking into a river, and she saw herself as a workhorse that could pull him to safety.

Ruby tried countless tactics to change Firoz's mind. She spent hours researching infidelity, Alim strapped to her back as she perused books in the self-help section of bookstores. She gifted Firoz with books like *A Couple's Guide to Finding the Love You Want; Infidelity: An Addiction; Affairs: A Guide to Working Through the Repercussions of Infidelity.* Ruby even suggested they start couples therapy. "We can work through this. I know we can," she urged. "The first step is admitting the problem." But Firoz would not budge. He denied her accusations and offered a slew of counter-arguments. "God, Ruby! With all that I have to worry about at the store, this is the last thing I need. Who knew you'd be such a handful?"

"Please, Firoz! Don't do this," Ruby wanted to yell, but she refused to beg or cry as many women she knew did, giving in so easily to their emotions. She pressed on, certain that her rational approach would be the one that he would understand—if not now, then in good time. But there were some days when Ruby was exhausted by efforts. It was as if Firoz had become too heavy, his weight uprooting her and pulling her down into the river with him. On those days, she would retreat briefly, but return soon after, with even greater energy.

Then one evening as Ruby lay on the couch watching Oprah, she had an epiphany. An "aha moment," as Oprah would call it. "When you can't steer your life where you want it to go, don't give up—learn to surrender," the guest psychologist said. "Learn to find the power to let go." Oprah piped in enthusiastically, "It's true, people. It is a principle that rules my life—knowing when to surrender. Surrendering doesn't mean letting go of your responsibility. You gotta do your part—only *you* have the power to change the direction of your life."

In that moment Ruby realized that she had been wasting her time trying to make Firoz change. She couldn't control him! What she had to do was focus on the things she could impact, places where she would have the greatest influence. Ruby spent the evening weighing her options, carefully outlining them in a notebook. How arrogant to think that I could have had it all! Ruby decided that she would accept Firoz's affairs—they were, she told herself, a compromise of motherhood. There was nothing more important in her life than Alim, and she would not raise him the way she had been raised. It was her job as a mother, Ruby decided, to break this cycle, not to carry it forward into the next generation. She vowed that night to create a stable environment for him, one in which he would always feel safe and secure, free of harm. Everything else was secondary.

With Ruby's newfound attitude, the fighting subsided. It was as if she and Firoz had come to the end of a tug-of-war. There was some satisfaction, or at least some relief, in it. Their new arrangement allowed Ruby to focus on her top priorities—building her business, and spending more time with Alim.

"You have to pick your battles," Ruby now says to herself in the bathroom mirror each morning as a way of reminding herself of where she should put her energy. She'd learned the technique during a sales leadership course in Puerto Rico—a reward for top-producing agents in the country. During one session, participants were encouraged to give themselves pep talks each morning. "It is a technique," the facilitator, a world-renowned motivational speaker, said, "that has a proven track record." Many of the most successful business people—people like Donald Trump, Martha Stewart, and Bill Gates—are reported to do just that each and every morning.

Now Ruby organizes various materials on the dining room table, such as a guest registry (which serves the dual purpose of monitoring visitors and providing her with a list of potential clients), feature sheets on which she's stapled her business cards, and information packages about the area. She then walks to the kitchen, slips the video into the TV–VCR sitting on the kitchen counter. It's the perfect spot. From here, the electrical towers are visible. Ruby then sets the eight-minute video on a loop so that it will play continuously through the afternoon.

Ruby supervised the video project closely and insisted that she be involved in writing the script as well as choosing details such as Dwayne's wardrobe. "You look great! The Approachable Expert—exactly what I wanted." Ruby said to him when he arrived at 314 Sunset on the day of the shoot in dark blue jeans and a brown corduroy jacket (which she had to buy) over a plaid shirt.

"Not like I had much choice," Dwayne retorted, and then followed her into the house.

The video, entitled *Electrical Towers: Nothing to Fear,* shows clips of interviews with people in the neighbourhood affirming their confidence in the area, interwoven with quick scientific facts. In one clip, Dwayne circles an electrical tower with a Gauss meter. A close-up shows the audience the meter reading. He repeats the process around a microwave, a cordless phone, a cell phone, a computer, and a smoke detector. "As you can see, there are many other sources of electromagnetic radiation in our everyday lives—and all of them are harmless. X-rays and MRIs expose us to much more radiation than electrical towers ever would." Dwayne then goes on to explain that electrical towers, like many household appliances, operate at the radio-frequency part of the electromagnetic spectrum—a non-ionizing radiation. Unlike X-rays and gamma rays, they do not have the energy to break the bonds that hold molecules in cells together and cause any damage. He had not wanted to include all these scientific facts, worried that people would feel overwhelmed: "It's not like we're dealing with Chernobyl here."

But Ruby insisted. "Buyers are sophisticated these days. They need to understand the science. It's the only way to put their minds at rest."

"Whatever you say, boss-lady," Dwayne said, shrugging. "It's your money. You do what you want with it."

"By the way, Dwayne, make sure you mention the differences between the ionized and non-ionized part of the electromagnetic spectrum. I think that's going to be the key to making people understand."

Dwayne raised his eyebrows. "How the heck do you know this stuff?"

Ruby was both irritated and pleased to see the shock on Dwayne's face. "I'm a scientist by training. A biochemist actually."

In England, Ruby had completed her undergraduate degree in biochemistry and was studying to be an optometrist when her parents insisted that she and Shelina return to Arusha, where they could apply as a family for their Green Cards to Canada. Shelina was fifteen and Ruby had not yet turned twenty-one, the maximum age a child could be included on the same application as her parents. There was no time to waste. They did not want to stay in Tanzania anymore—the political situation continued to worsen. "Better to leave with something than nothing at all." Ruby's parents, like so many others, did not want to try for England. It was in deep recession, and with Thatcher newly in power—not to mention the increased activity of skinheads—many were pessimistic about their future in that country. At the same time, stories started circulating—not only in England but in East Africa also—of the many Ismailis who had struck it rich in Canada, people like the Hashams who had made it big in the hotel business, or the Bogas in jeans and T-shirts. The Canadian economy was strong—especially in provinces like Alberta and Ontario—and Trudeau's government was encouraging immigration.

Soon, discussions at dinner tables, in the social halls of jamatkhanas, or during games of badminton, turned to Canada. People hurried to apply for immigration. The process was long, and it could take years before you were granted your Green Card. Jamatkhanas like the one in Ilford—the first one in the U.K.—started emptying out as the exodus began, yet again, but this time to Canada. In Tanzania and Kenya, the same was true. The only difference was that the jamat there had already shrunk in numbers, many having fled only a few years earlier, worried about the mounting hostility toward Asians, which in Uganda had led to Idi Amin's expulsion order.

For months and even years to come, words of congratulation could be heard at the many jamatkhanas as people shared their stories of a successful application. "Got our Green Cards today.

Shukar Mowla!" And for those who were still waiting, words of encouragement, *Inshallah,* and for those who'd been rejected, often because they had failed their medicals or were deemed to have undesirable occupations—Canada understandably preferred professionals—words of consolation. "Ah, not to worry. This is God's country."

"But my degree will be wasted!' Ruby said to her parents in protest, even if that was not the only reason she hadn't wanted to leave England. She was in love with Malik, a classmate at The London Eye Hospital whom she had been secretly dating for almost a year. (She didn't want to set a bad example for Shelina.) Luckily, Malik's parents, who were already in England, were keen on migrating to Canada also. It was only a matter of time before they would be together again.

"A biochemist? No shit." Dwayne said, smiling as if he had discovered a tantalizing secret. "Somehow I can't picture you in a lab, you know? Flasks, test tubes, microscopes? No way. Seems too dull for the kind of lady you are."

How do you know who I am? Ruby wanted to say, but didn't. She often wondered why people found it so hard to believe that you can be more than just one thing. "Did my final paper on *The Half-Life of Unstable Elements,"* she said as if to prove herself.

"Is that like the unstable molecules of Captain Marvel? The Fantastic Four? The Invisible Woman?" Dwayne joked.

"Not at all," Ruby said in an authoritative tone. She had no idea whom he was referring to, but was offended that he was comparing her work to what sounded like comic book characters. "Unstable elements don't have a full orbit of electrons and decay faster. That's the crux of it."

"God Lord, lady. You put all of us regular fellas to shame. A real estate agent, a scientist. Is there anything you can't do?" he asked, winking.

Ruby ignored Dwayne's comment and set him to work. But for a moment she thought about her career path. She had never planned on being a real estate agent, but her degree in biochemistry was not recognized in Canada. She only received partial credit for her courses, which seemed ridiculous to Ruby, given that the Canadian curriculum was much easier than the British one. If she wanted to pursue optometry—or anything else in the sciences—she would have to redo her undergraduate degree. Moreover, there was only one Canadian university that offered optometric training in English, and Waterloo was on the other side of the country, which might as well be the other side of the world. This was not England. Ruby did not want to leave her parents. They were new to the country, not to mention living in the West. They would need her. And Shelina was too young. Family friends suggested she become a medical laboratory technologist, which was a two-year program at SAIT. But Ruby wanted a career that would challenge her, not one in which she would be relegated to mundane tasks like examining medical swabs, or blood and urine samples, leaving the real work to the doctors.

Ruby enrolled in Business School at the University of Calgary and majored in information systems. Many other Ismaili students were studying computers in one form or another, and she decided to do the same. It was in her mind a practical degree, and one that would serve her and her family well. Ironically, when Ruby graduated from the University of Calgary with what was now her second degree she could not find a job. By then, the Canadian economy had slowed. At that time, Ruby felt angry and cheated, but it didn't take long for her to put the disappointment behind her and focus on what had to be done. Now, when she looks back, she says to herself, See, everything always turns out for the best.

In the hall mirror, Ruby checks her hair, which has been blow-dried straight and coloured with L'Oréal D4 (Ash Blonde), turning it from its natural dark brown to a shade of caramel. She then reapplies her lipstick—burnt cocoa—and places a tissue between her lips to remove the excess. When she bends down and rubs a thumb over the tip of her black pumps, she notices a run in her pantyhose. "Oh, shoot, look at this," she says to herself, and snaps the nylon against her skin.

Outside, Ruby steps over the chalked outline of a body and retrieves a package of Secret pantyhose from the trunk of the car, pulling the right shade from a box filled with other personal items such as sticks of deodorant and mouthwash. She then slams the trunk shut and heads back to the house. In the bathroom, she quickly removes her old nylons and changes into the new ones. As she reaches in to adjust the waistband of her underwear, she notices her C-section scar, which has always looked to Ruby like a fading smile. During childbirth, Ruby had dilated to ten centimetres, but Alim still would not drop, stubbornly staying well above the birth canal. Ruby had wanted to have a natural birth, but after twenty-four hours' labour, she had no choice but to agree to a Caesarean section. "Like mother, like son," Firoz would say, shaking his head, whenever he recounted the story at dinner parties. Now, as Ruby rushes back downstairs to wait for potential buyers, she remembers the pain of climbing stairs after Alim's birth. "Why don't you just ask me if you need something from upstairs," Firoz had coaxed. But Ruby refused, saying the only way to heal was to push through the pain.

"Here, let me help you," Ruby says to a woman as she struggles to manoeuvre her stroller through the front door. The woman smiles and thanks her.

Ruby bends down to inspect the child, a little girl with a mass of blonde curls, her doll dangling outside the stroller. "Oh, she's adorable! They're so great at this age, aren't they?" Ruby says as she tucks the doll, whose face has been scribbled on with a black marker, back into the child's hands. "Here you go, sweetie."

Ruby knows that it is important to take the time to speak to each visitor individually, even if many are not serious—for many aren't. They might be neighbours taking advantage of the opportunity to see the house or people passing their afternoon—much as she used to. Ruby also enjoys talking to each person, getting to know them, if only briefly.

Ruby gives the woman an overview of the house. "You go ahead, take a boo. I'll take care of the stroller."

"Are you sure?" the woman asks as she leans down and scoops her child out of the stroller.

"Of course. Years of experience," Ruby says, and winks. The woman smiles approvingly.

As Ruby expertly collapses the stroller and leans it against the wall, her mind travels back to when Alim was a baby. It was now her trying to manoeuvre a stroller, this time through snow and ice. She was on maternity leave from AGT, Alberta Government Telephones, where she worked as a customer service representative. She had taken the job after graduation, as a temporary measure, until the economy picked up again and she could pursue a career in Information Technology. On many afternoons, Ruby would bundle Alim into his bulky snowsuit and then lug him through the city by bus to attend an Open House. They only had one car and Firoz needed it to deliver orders at the store, which was still a fledgling enterprise at the time. Personal delivery was, they both agreed, a good way to differentiate Firoz's shop from the many other copy shops that seemed to be popping up throughout the city.

Ruby wasn't interested in buying a house then. She and Firoz already owned a townhouse in Whitehorn, and it would take years before they would be able to buy a bigger house, and one in a nicer area—like the one they live in now, a four-level split in Lake Bonaventure. Instead, she attended Open Houses, partly as a way to get out of the house, which at times seemed to close in on her, and partly as a way of passing her days, which often seemed endless with Firoz at the store all day, and not returning until late. Who knew he wasn't always at work?

There had been something thrilling for Ruby about being in other people's homes. She felt as if she was cheating in some way, as if she'd entered a movie theatre without paying—not that she'd ever do that. As she toured each house, she watched real estate agents interacting with potential buyers, listened in on their conversations, and in each instance, Ruby knew that she could do a better job. She felt that many of them had no idea what it took to be a good salesperson. They focused on razzle-dazzling clients, smooth-talking their way over problems. No doubt presentation was important! Ruby knew that. But she also knew that there was another skill that was even more important—listening.

At AGT, Ruby spent her days listening to customers, many of whom were calling in to lodge a complaint. Ruby was a natural at it and was able to efficiently handle a large call volume. People felt at ease with her, as if they could tell her anything, even their darkest secrets. In fact, her boss regularly used Ruby as a benchmark. He would play her conversations with customers, taped for quality assurance, to the department during training seminars, pointing out her skills—skills that Ruby had never thought were particularly special, until she realized, years later during these

Open Houses, what she could use them for. When Ruby announced to Firoz that she wanted to pursue a career in real estate, he encouraged her, but at the same he warned her: "Don't expect too much—it's not like working for the government, you know. It's tough being in business for yourself. Look at how much I'm struggling with the store."

The woman with the baby returns after touring the house. "Beautiful place," she says, adjusting her child on her hip.

Ruby engages her, drawing her out expertly, but the woman is only looking. Ruby smiles and then provides her with an overview of her sales record. "With a growing family, you never know when you'll need a new house. Please, call me if I can help in any way." Ruby hands her a business card and then helps with the stroller as the woman leaves.

It's close to the end of the afternoon and Ruby hasn't had many visitors, but her spirits buoy when she sees a couple and their teenage daughter approaching the front door. "Please come in." As Ruby holds the screen door open, she catches a glimpse of a white poodle across the street, hobbling up a set of porch steps, its back leg in a bandage.

Ruby learns that Francie and Thom Silverberg are here for the week from Toronto with their daughter, Lucy. Francie works for a hotel chain, and the company, like so many others, has recently relocated its headquarters to Calgary. Thom is a computer analyst and is confident that he will find a job once they move here. After all, Calgary's economy is booming.

"We can't wait to get here. Slow down our lives. We've had it up to here with big-city life," Francie says, her hand slicing the air under her chin. "It's a rat race in Toronto."

"Quite the opposite here," Ruby says with a broad smile. "This city is perfect! Low crime. Low pollution. Low taxes. No wonder it's been ranked as one of the most livable cities in the world."

Francie smiles knowingly and then goes on to list the many reasons they don't like Toronto. The pollution (Try breathing on a humid day—impossible.), the traffic (Oh God, the traffic.), the violence (Might as well live in the States.), the poor city planning (Who puts a highway in front of the lake? Not that it matters, can't swim in it. It's a sewer.).

"Exactly!" Thom says, putting his arm around Lucy. "*This* is the place to raise a family."

Ruby turns and smiles at Lucy, who is dressed in tight jeans with cuts like gashes running up and down the legs, and a bright yellow T-shirt with asymmetrical sleeves and a partially frayed hem. "Very cool T-shirt. Are you a fan of the Rolling Stones?"

Lucy shrugs and looks away.

"It's reconstructed vintage," Thom explains, pulling his daughter closer to him. "Actually used to be mine."

"Really? My husband's a big fan of the Rolling Stones too."

"Ah, them were the days, weren't they?"

"They sure were," Ruby says, smiling, as she remembers Firoz trying to sing "Ruby Tuesday" to her during what he had called their first anniversary. "Anniversary? What are you talking about?" Ruby asked. They weren't dating. "I can't believe you don't remember, *mera pyar!*" Firoz retorted, clutching his heart with false exaggeration. "We met exactly one year ago today, Ruby Tuesday." Ruby laughed but still made him stop. "Aye, you're so strict," Firoz said, shaking his head and smiling. "Exactly the kind of girl I need!" From then on he refrained from singing the song, but he would still hum it to her and continued calling her by this nickname.

Ruby directs the Silverbergs to the guest registry, and as she waits for them to tour the house, she finds herself thinking about Firoz. They met at university, where he too was in the faculty of business, but he was studying marketing. He had asked her out on numerous occasions, but she refused each time. She enjoyed his company and he was no doubt charming and quite intelligent, but she did not find him attractive. Besides, she was taken and told him so. She didn't want to lead him on. "I have a boyfriend," she told him flatly. "Practically engaged actually." "Well, there's nothing wrong in being friends is there?" he asked. "Or is your boyfriend the controlling type?"

Ruby was quite lonely. She didn't have many friends yet. She'd found it difficult blending in with other Ismailis—many of whom had been here for almost a decade now and acted as if they owned every inch of Canada. Also, Shelina was in high school and leading, it seemed, a separate life. Soon, Ruby and Firoz started to spend more and more time together. They studied together regularly—often in Reserve, the basement of the Main Library, where many other Ismaili students could also be found. But more often than not they took up an entire table to themselves. Firoz lived on campus—his family was in Edmonton—and so they often ate dinner at the cafeteria in his building, or else took their trays upstairs and ate in the TV lounge while watching shows like *Jeopardy*, in which Ruby would inadvertently beat him each time. "You're way too smart for me," Firoz would tease. "How in the world can I compete with you?"

Through it all, Ruby and Malik spoke regularly—and for that matter Firoz also dated other women, even if he would on occasion try to hold Ruby's hand, or even kiss her. In fact, he'd always aim for her lips, instead of her cheek, when he congratulated her on Kushali or Eid. Malik had taken up a part-time job to pay for their phone calls. He and Ruby also wrote to each other obsessively, his letters arriving at a post office box. Soon, the good news Ruby was expecting finally arrived. Malik's family had received their Green Cards!

But strangely, shortly after Malik arrived, Ruby realized that she was in love with Firoz. It was as if Malik's presence acted like photo-solution poured on a negative, crystallizing her feelings and bringing them to the surface. Ruby found herself thinking about Firoz constantly and she could not imagine her life without him. She apologized to Malik, but said she had to follow her heart. "I'll never forgive you!" Malik said before storming out of Denny's restaurant.

When Ruby confessed her love to Firoz, he just smiled and pulled her in to him. "I knew you'd come around. It was only a matter of time. Love, it's like a runaway train, don't you think? There's just no stopping it."

Firoz broke up with his then girlfriend and Ruby and he were married a year later in 1983 during the Imam's Silver Jubilee. Firoz wore a tuxedo rented from Malabar, and Ruby, a white satin gown. They lined up behind hundreds of other couples, eager for their few moments with the Imam. The ceremonies took place at the Max Bell Arena, which had been turned overnight into a beautiful celebration hall by thousands of volunteers. Both of them had been so nervous, their hands shaking in front of them—not because it was their wedding day—they were confident in each other—but because neither one of them had ever been in such close proximity to the Imam before. After the ceremonies, Firoz's mother blessed them, placing their heads together and wishing them a long, prosperous life together. If it rained on your wedding day it was a good omen. It was April and outside it was snowing. "A Canadian version of good luck, hanh?" she joked and then dabbed her eyes with the end of her sari.

Malik is an optometrist specializing in laser eye surgery, and now lives in Toronto. He is married to a friend of theirs from Ilford jamatkhana, Faiza, and they have three children, two boys and a girl. On the rare nights that Firoz reaches for Ruby, she lets her mind travel back to England and she imagines that it is Malik, not her husband, who is moving over her.

The Silverbergs return from the tour. They like the house— the set-up is perfect for them. Thom loves the built-in barbeque

and fire pit, Francie loves the view, and Lucy, the finished basement, which will be hers.

"But we're concerned about the electrical towers. Honestly,
I'm not sure I would have thought about it until I saw the video."

Francie's comment jars Ruby at first, but she recovers quickly,
her mind clearing a path to a possible solution. "Me too," Ruby
says confidently. "That's exactly the problem, you see. There's
been a lot of media attention on the towers, and that's scared
people even when all the facts show that there's no need to be. It's
the only reason this house hasn't sold. It's a real find. There's no
way a house like this should be listed at such a low price. But it's
amazing what people will focus on when they're scared. And the
ironic thing is that media will bore with this issue soon enough
and move on to a new way of scaring us."

"So true. It's ridiculous really. Do they expect us to believe
them anymore?" Francie says, crossing her arms. She then cites
other examples of the media blowing things out of proportion.
Mad cow disease. Global warming. Asian flu.

"This house is really like a fixer-upper. Do you know what
I mean?" Ruby asks, aware that a significant percentage of
Toronto's real estate market is made up of older homes or ones
that are rundown. "You have to be able to see past the fact that it
needs some work—but of course not everyone can. And the ones
who do—well, they're usually sitting on a gold mine."

Francie nods enthusiastically. "Of course! Toronto is filled
with people like that."

"Buy low. Renovate. Sell high," Thom says, shaking his head. "Another good reason to get out of there. Everything's too damn expensive."

Francie then tells Ruby about the many people who bought houses in areas called Trinity-Bellwoods and Parkdale. "No one wanted to buy there a couple of years ago. Everyone was scared off by the mental hospital in the area."

"And now their houses are worth an insane amount—no pun intended," Thom adds, laughing. "You had to get in early, that's the thing."

"Well, you can get in early here," Ruby says, making direct eye contact with Thom and then Francie. "All this house needs is someone who can look past the electrical tower to the opportunity."

Francie raises her eyebrows. "Do you think there's any room to negotiate?"

"I can tell you that the buyers are motivated to sell, that's for sure," Ruby says, excited by the inroads she's making. Just then, her cell phone rings and when she flips it open, she sees from the caller ID that it's Lynda and Lance. "Speak of the devil," Ruby says with a wink. "Should I tell them we have an interested party?"

Francie and Thom look at each other. "Sure, why not? But we still want to see a few more houses."

"Of course. Only natural." The Nickels are thrilled with Ruby's news—it's the first bite they've had since they listed the property. When she hangs up, Ruby waves her cell phone in the air. "Even this thing emits radiation!"

Francie and Thom laugh. "Remember when hair dryers were supposed to cause cancer?" Francie asks.

Ruby makes arrangements to call them later this evening. She also offers them free passes to various tourist spots like the Calgary Tower and Calaway Park. "It'll make the trip more enjoyable," she says, cocking her head toward Lucy, who is sitting in the family room flipping through *O* magazine.

Thom and Francie smile, and Ruby feels hopeful that she will sell the house before the end of the weekend.

RUBY PACKS UP and then quickly walks through the house to make sure everything is in order. In the kitchen, she ejects the video, touching it to her forehead like a talisman before sliding it into her satchel. She turns off the coffee maker and rinses the carafe, then places it in the sink. From the window above the sink, she looks into the backyard and sees the base of the electrical tower. Ruby cranes her neck, but she still can't see the top of the tower. It's as if the top has been lopped off. A headless giant. Ruby feels the need to see the entire tower, to see what she has just conquered, brought down to the ground.

Ruby slides open the patio door and steps out onto the deck. She hears a cat yowling behind the fence that separates the yard from the neighbours', and from the corner of her eye, she spots fragments of the animal between the slats. As Ruby approaches the electrical tower, the ground beneath her feels soft, the grass wet from an earlier rain shower. The heels of her shoes dig into the lawn, creating a line of tiny pockmarks from the deck to the tower.

At the tower, Ruby hangs her head back and is suddenly amazed by its size, the sheer immensity of it. She circles the tower, waving her hand back and forth, as if to see if she can feel the electromagnetic force field. How ridiculous! she says to herself, laughing at the absurdity of her actions. Ruby then leans her body against the tower, pushing at it as she would a stalled car, expecting it to move somehow. But of course it doesn't. It stands there, fixed. Ruby's leg shoots out, ready to kick the tower, but then she catches herself and quickly sets her foot back on the ground. She turns away and focuses her gaze on the city below. The view really is spectacular. The valley, the snaking roads, the mountains. The city is a well-organized grid, the four quadrants neatly portioned into neighbourhoods like pieces of a birthday cake.

In the distance, Ruby notices another electrical tower. It looks minuscule, the size of a candle, as if it's part of a scale-model of the city. From here it's hard to imagine that it rises hundreds of feet above the earth. As Ruby examines the city, she suddenly begins to see more and more towers. They are everywhere—as if the city is an electrical field! But there is no pattern to their location. They seem to be randomly dispersed. There are some houses with several towers nearby, while others have only one or two, and yet others have none. Why didn't the city have a plan? Ruby wants to know. It's as if the city never once considered that the towers might be harmful. But what if they are? Ruby asks herself for the first time. She feels a strange bitterness rise in her, like an unexpected aftertaste. Ruby wants to spit it out, but instead she swallows hard and then turns to leave. She has to get home. She still has work to do.

Samuel Mathews

The stewardess, in her tight green uniform, extended her arm over the seats in front of us and leaned in. "Drinks?" she asked in a Swedish accent.

I sat in the window seat, fidgeting with excitement. I had never been on an airplane before. It was August of 1975 and I was seven years old. It was hard to believe, but overnight, we would be transported to a new world. It was as if we were climbing into a storybook where we would easily become part of the page. For months now, my father had told me all that Canada offered and I could not wait to get there. He sat in the middle seat, and my mother in the aisle seat. This way she could attend to my dadima, my father's mother, who sat in the row behind us. My dadima refused anyone's help except my mother's. It was, after all, my mother's duty as her daughter-in-law to attend to all her needs.

The stewardess reached over to release our meal trays and then snapped open three Coca-Cola bottles. My mother leaned into the aisle, twisting her head back, and translated for my dadima. She wanted a cup of tea. After the stewardess left, my dadima tapped my mother's arm. "Eh-hey, Shamim, call that hussy back. I want saccharine, not sugar. And ask for more cashews. As if such a small package will fill me up."

My dadima had a long list of ailments, none of which I understood. All I knew was that she carried a pillbox of multicoloured tablets and a small flask of brandy in an oversized black purse, which she clicked open every few minutes to check the contents. "She's crazy, I swear," I once heard my mother say to her sister. "Not like she carries any money in there. Thinks we're made of gold."

"How about a colouring book?" the stewardess asked when she returned with my dadima's saccharine. She waved a plastic package at me.

I nodded enthusiastically. The stewardess handed me the package. Inside, I found a set of crayons and a colouring book titled *Vinter Olympisk 1976: Innsbruck Willkommen die Welt!* The cover featured a downhill skier in a sleek red snowsuit, one leg splayed back as he pushed himself through the starting gate.

My dadima tapped my mother's elbow. "Eh-hey, Shamim. *Mukaye-pasab laygee-ai.* I need the washroom." My dadima could go to the washroom by herself, but preferred assistance. She was a bulky woman and often had trouble removing her underwear and properly aligning herself over the toilet seat.

My mother rolled her eyes and then unbuckled her seat belt.

"Looks like fun, huh, Farah?" my father asked me, tapping his pen on the skier's goggles.

"Uh-huh," I said.

My father was an avid athlete. Fit body, fit mind, he would always say. In Nairobi, he went speed walking each weekday morning at 5 A.M., circling the track at the Aga Khan Sports Club until the sun rose at 6 A.M. My mother would not allow me to go with him; it was too early and I was too young. But I insisted on golfing with him each Saturday at the Royal Nairobi Golf Club, where I was the only child on the course, not to mention, the only girl. I could barely carry my golf clubs and I inevitably slowed his game. But my father never said anything. He waited patiently as I swung the ball, moving it forward a few feet at a time, scoring triple and quadruple *boogies,* while he scored birdies and pars, even eagles. His swing was smooth and sure. I watched him carefully, eager to shadow his every move.

"Maybe we'll go skiing in Canada," he said. "Too cold to golf."

"Is this Canada?" I asked, examining the cover.

"No, it's Austria," he laughed. "But close enough." My father went on to explain that the Winter Olympics were being held in Innsbruck the following year even though they were originally supposed to have been held in Denver, Colorado. "But the Americans, they didn't plan properly, you see. Let things get out of hand. Hard to believe, really. Think they're so bloody smart and still they ran out of money," my father said, shaking his head. "So what do you think? Should we take up skiing?"

"Yes!" I emptied the crayons onto my meal tray.

My father removed his To Do list from his shirt pocket and added a new item, *Ski Lessons*. He had started the list months before, adding and removing items as our impending departure neared. At the top of the list, in red ink: *Find a Business*. My father had six brothers and sisters. He was not the eldest son, but it was still his job to set up a business in Canada, get us settled as quickly as possible, and then sponsor the rest of the family. He had dreams of studying abroad, but when my grandfather died of unknown reasons during a trip to Rangoon, leaving my dadima a widow at the age of thirty-six, my father took over the family business as well as the responsibility of the family. He was sixteen years old.

His brother Kamru was the eldest at nineteen, but he was unaccustomed to working. He had been the first to benefit from my grandfather's business success, the *nouveau riche* of Kenya. He was spoiled and spent most of his time at the casino or in bars. My father built the family business to new heights. "You have the Midas touch," people told him. Years later, my father accidentally found out through a business acquaintance that my grandfather was not dead; he was remarried and now living in

Hyderabad. My father never told his family. There was no point in causing them any undue pain.

My parents had had no plans of leaving Kenya, but the combination of Nyerere's nationalization scheme in Tanzania followed by the expulsion of Asians in Uganda sent one shock wave after another through the Asian community in East Africa. It's only a matter of time, people said, before Kenyatta follows suit. It was as if we had been swept into the ocean, our feet no longer able to reach the bottom. Many scrambled to invest abroad. But my father already had an escape plan. He had been sending money out of the country for years through my mother's cousin-brother, Jimmy Ratansi, or Jimmy Bond as my father would sometimes call him, winking at my mother and saying, "Kenya's top secret agent, nuh?" to which my mother would just smile or at other times, cuff his elbow and then scold him, half laughing. "Shh! Your mother will hear."

Jimmy Uncle was an exporter of coffee and had accounts overseas. My father arranged to give him cash shillings, which he used to pay his workers and buy supplies. Jimmy Uncle then transferred money from his account to one in London that he had opened for my father under the name Samuel Mathews, an alias for my father, whose name is Shiraz Mitha. Jimmy Uncle wanted to pay my father a rate that was better than the black market rate, but my father refused. "As if I could do that. You're my brother now."

Jimmy Uncle was the only boy in a family filled with girls. He also had a severe limp (having had polio as a child), which served to generate excessive sympathy from his sisters and cousin-sisters. My mother asked my father to please help Jimmy Uncle; he had been involved in several businesses, all of which had failed. "If you don't help him, God only knows what will happen to him," she said. Jimmy Uncle was older than my father and still had not made his mark in the world. My father agreed to help. He encouraged Jimmy Uncle to get into the coffee business. Many in the community had begun to diversify, to invest in new businesses like manufacturing and farming. After all, owning a shop made you vulnerable; it built resentment among Africans. My father taught Jimmy Uncle how to manage his business. It was important, for instance, not to report all your income. This would help minimize taxes. It was also important to keep a tight reign on employees—otherwise they'd rob you blind. With the combination of my father's sound business advice and rising world coffee prices, Jimmy Uncle's business flourished. Soon, he became a rich man, and many women, who had normally ignored him, were now pursuing him left, right, and centre.

"How to know? Are they well intentioned or are they only after my money?" Jimmy Uncle asked my father when he came over for tea. "I wish I was lucky like you, Shiraz-*bhai*."

"What luck?" my father said, smiling at my mother. "I just made a good choice."

Jimmy Uncle laid his cane across his lap. "No, no. Even if you choose, who knows what she will turn out to be like in the end. I'm telling you, it all depends on your luck, your *naseeb*."

"You're right, Jimmy," my mother teased as she poured him another cup of tea. "He's lucky that I even gave him a chance."

"See that?" my father said, his palms to the air. "See how she treats me? Maybe you're the lucky one, Jimmy Bond. Better not to be trapped by the love of a woman. Once they have you, *kalas*—you're done for. You'll take anything she throws your way."

Everyone laughed, including me, although I didn't think it was funny. To me, it was romantic. I did not fully understand what my father meant, but in my mind, I saw him effortlessly carrying anything my mother threw at him—pots, pans, balls and bats. There was nothing he would not do for her.

My parents had a love marriage, which was still unusual in those days and made me feel special. We were not like other families. We were a modern family. The idea of love, free love, had trickled into Kenya through Hollywood movies, magazines, business trips to London, and people returning after studying abroad. If you looked at early photographs of my parents, my father is wearing bell-bottoms and platform shoes. His hair is styled (and still is) like Elvis's, his dark locks slicked up and back with Yardley's. My mother is wearing cork-heeled sandals under a mini-skirt, she has black, thick-rimmed eyeglasses on, and her hair is styled in a beehive. To my dadima's dismay, my parents also held hands in public and were often seen arm in arm. "Shameless! She'll ruin our reputation, that girl will." My mother was also the same age as my father (twenty-two when they met), not to mention the fact that she was much too educated: she had attended Kianda College of Secretarial Management and was working as a bookkeeper at the Hilton. "Mark my words. She will never take care of you properly." My father ignored my dadima's pleas. "Love is enough," my father told his mother, to which she cried and beat her chest. "Love? What kind of rubbish are you talking? You think that is what makes a marriage work? You wait and see. That girl will be the end of us one day."

My mother's parents approved of my father. This is the way of the new world, isn't it? Let the children choose what will make them happy. My mother had five older sisters and by the time she was of age, her parents were tired—she would joke—of trying to find yet another suitable match. Thank God! Even so, her parents insisted, as was the custom, that a chaperone accompany them on their dates. Jimmy Uncle was chosen and for close to a year, he would trail behind them during their walks, even bring a book along and wait in the car, or else join them at Kenya Cinema but watch another film, or even go to a friend's house, where my parents would pick him up at the end of the evening.

Jimmy Uncle finally made a choice and married a woman confined to a wheelchair. This way, he had said, she would never leave him, even if his luck turned bad and he lost all his money.

"Don't be silly, Jimmy," my mother said as she refilled his cup with tea. "If anything ever happened, as if we're not here for you. That's what family is for."

After returning from the washroom and buckling my dadima back into her seat, my mother leaned over and whispered to my father, "My God, it's like having a baby." She then explained that the airplane washrooms were so small that she had had to leave the door open, asking one of the stewardesses to watch for other passengers. "I swear the woman should be in diapers."

My father nodded and took her hand in his. "Take it easy, darling. It won't be long until Kamru moves to Canada." In Nairobi, my dadima used to live with Kamru Uncle. Kamru Uncle was unmarried, so my dadima had no choice but to accept the ayah he'd hired. To my mother's consternation, my father's family decided it was better if my dadima immigrated with us rather than waiting to immigrate with Kamru Uncle. The sooner she got to Canada the better. After all, the Canadian health system was much more reliable (not to mention free). "If something ever happened to her," my father's siblings had said to him, "God knows, you would never be able to forgive yourself."

AFTER REGISTERING ME in grade two at Connaught Elementary School, my parents set out looking for an apartment. They found several, but in the end, my father decided on the one that was slightly more expensive. "Are you sure, darling?" my mother asked. "Absolutely," my father said. The apartment was a modest two-bedroom at the edge of Calgary's downtown core. The appliances were mismatched, the walls were watermarked, but it had a balcony. My father wanted my mother to be able to grow her flowers—even if only in the summer. Our flat in Nairobi had had a back garden and a front verandah, both of which boasted brilliant pink and red flowers. My mother scrubbed the pigeon droppings off the balcony and then decorated it with a few pots of hardy plants, ones capable of enduring the winter. "Looks so pretty," I said. "It certainly does, doesn't it, *mitu?*" my mother responded. "But this is just temporary, you know. Wait 'til your father finds a business. Then we'll move into a proper house with a garden and everything."

Our apartment doubled as my father's office and I was now privy to conversations that would never have taken place in front of me in Nairobi. My father spent most of his time at the kitchen table, a foldaway that my parents had purchased at The Bay and set up at the end of the small galley kitchen. He would flip through the classified sections of Alberta's newspapers—*Calgary Herald, Edmonton Journal, Red Deer Advocate, Olds Gazette*—circling potential ads under the column Businesses for Sale. On the wall behind the kitchen table, he had tacked a large wall map of Alberta, the various towns decorated with red and green push-pins. "Too bad we hadn't come earlier, huh?" my father once joked. "Like the British—those smart bastards! Then we would-n't have to worry about finding a business. We would have found all this land instead. Not to mention, we would have made real Indians out of the Indians, huh?"

Each day after school, I would rush home, eager as always to tell my father about my day. He was usually busy working at the kitchen table, but when I came in, his attention always turned to me. My dadima often sat at the table with him—to give him company, as she put it, even though my mother was only a few feet away preparing our dinner. My mother made two different meals, one for us and one for my dadima, who needed to control her sugar and salt intake. There weren't any proper Indian grocery shops in Calgary yet, but my mother had brought a box from Nairobi that was packed with spices, as well as a bronze mortar and pestle that had been her mother's. "Your mother, she's a saint. What would we do without her, huh?" my father would often say at the end of a meal.

"Come look at this," he said to me one day when I came home from school.

I threw my lunch kit and Etch-a-Sketch by the front door and hurried to him. The Etch-a-Sketch was a welcoming gift from Shirin Virji, a woman my mother had befriended at jamatkhana. There were hardly any Ismailis in Canada yet, especially in Calgary; most of them had settled in Toronto or Vancouver. (My parents had chosen Alberta because of its good business climate. They also liked the idea of living close to the Rockies. They had spent part of their honeymoon in Moshi, at the base of Mount Kilimanjaro, and ever since had loved the mountains.) There were several makeshift jamatkhanas in Calgary, one held on weekdays at various people's houses (including one at the Nanjis' a few blocks away), and two others, held on weekends—one in a hall on Tenth Avenue and another one near the old airport. We didn't go to jamatkhana often. "What's the point of going," my mother had asked my father, "if I spend the whole time doing one thing or the other for the old woman?" My mother suggested that my father and I go to jamatkhana and she would stay home with my dadima. My father refused. He would not go without her. "It's okay, darling. We'll make our own *khane,* right here." So we did—we sat around the coffee table, on the orange shag carpet, saying both *du'as,* singing a *ginan,* and then reciting a *firman* each evening starting at seven. My dadima tried protesting. "What am I? A prisoner. Can't go anywhere. Keep me locked in this godforsaken place all day." "It's easier this way, Ma," my father explained, to which my dadima retorted, "Not everything in life has to be easy-*kama*-easy, understand? Sometimes, you have to suffer."

My father lifted me onto his lap. "See this," he said, running his finger up and down the ridges representing the Rockies on the map of Alberta. "This is where we'll go skiing."

"But when, Daddy? When are we going to go skiing?" I wasn't interested in skiing as much as I was in spending Saturdays with my father once again. Most of our weekends were now spent driving to various towns to look at businesses that were for sale.

"But isn't it dangerous?" my dadima asked as she slurped her tea. "Especially for a girl?"

"Can't be that dangerous. Thousands of people do it—both girls and boys," my mother said. She leaned down and removed a casserole dish of *keema* and *mayai* from the oven using two tea towels as oven mitts.

"Exactly, Ma. Shamim is right."

My dadima mumbled something and pushed her chair back. It screeched against the tile floor. "Eh-hey, Shamim. Washroom," she said as she pressed her palms to the table and lifted herself to standing.

My mother released the oven door and then placed the dish on the stovetop; the eggs, sunny-side-up, looked liked islands on top of the ground meat. She threw the tea towels onto the kitchen counter and then walked past my dadima. My dadima's long thin ponytail, which was spiraled into a twist and coloured with henna, swung from side to side as she followed.

"Can we go skiing soon?" I asked eagerly.

"Of course! We just have to wait for it to snow." My father removed a green push-pin from Ponoka and replaced it with a red one. Ponoka had been a bust. The business had looked good on paper, but when we had driven there the previous weekend in our newly purchased car, a used Chevy Impala, my father decided against it. A dry cleaner in a town of three thousand people, most of whom were farmers and probably owned only one suit, if that, seemed an unviable business. "Too bad we can't find a town filled with Ismailis," he joked. "Then surely a dry cleaner would be a booming business."

"But when, Daddy? When will it snow?"

"Soon, *mitu,* soon."

The next day, it snowed, confirming my father's status as my hero. He could do anything, even orchestrate the weather. Snow for me had existed only in fairy tales and to see it was magical. We were so excited that my father and I walked around our neighbourhood for hours, letting the snow collect on our hair, our lashes. Each day after, when I came home from school, we measured the accumulation of snow on our balcony. At first we used our fingers like dipping sticks (one digit, two digits), and later a ruler. I recorded our findings on a ruled piece of paper torn out of my math book and tacked next to my father's map of Alberta. We recorded the date, the amount of snow that day, and the cumulative amount. Soon, my father assured me, there would be enough snow for us to venture out to the mountains.

AFTER EXTENSIVE ANALYSIS and weighing of all his options, my father narrowed his search. He decided he would try to buy a Bottle Recycling Depot. True, it wasn't a glamorous business, he said, but the Alberta government issued limited permits, so if you were successful in obtaining one, it would mean a licence for printing money. A few weeks after the first snowfall, my father successfully obtained a licence for a bottle depot in Canmore, right in the Rocky Mountains. All he had to do now was have our money transferred from London. My father removed all the push-pins from his map and placed a gold-coloured thumbtack in Canmore. To celebrate, my mother made beef *biryani* and set the table with paper napkins, shaped into roses; my father brought home a tub of Neapolitan ice cream and a glossy brochure from the Canmore Ski Club. We all sat around the kitchen table eating straight from the container.

"We'll begin on a bunny hill," my father said as he reached to scrape out another spoonful of ice cream.

"With rabbits?"

"No, no," he laughed. He explained the different types of runs and then assured me that it wouldn't take us long to graduate from bunny hills to black diamond runs.

That evening, my father called his family in Nairobi and told them the good news. "We knew we could count on you," Kamru Uncle said. "You really do have the Midas touch."

"Better start packing," my father said, laughing.

"*Shukar Mowla,* thank God. We're finally set." My dadima wiped a smudge of ice cream off her lips using the back of her hand and then stood up. Her favourite TV show, *The Price Is Right*, was starting soon.

"Yes, start packing," my mother whispered, winking at my father, as my dadima walked to the living room.

When my father made arrangements to have our money transferred to Canada, the bank in London told him that they did not have any record of a Mr. Samuel Mathews. "What? Impossible!" my father said. "But I am him." He insisted that they double-check their records. This was obviously an accounting error. The bank asked for a paper trail so that they could launch an investigation. But my father did not have any records of the transactions. Jimmy Uncle did. It had been too risky to have the deposit slips mailed from London to Nairobi. After all, it was illegal to send money out of the country.

Instead, the slips were mailed to a post office box in London.

"Call that rascal right now," my dadima said. "God only knows what he's done with our money."

"Take it easy, Ma. It's the middle of the night there. Let's wait some." My father sat down at the kitchen table, placing his arm on a stack of newspapers.

"Just call him now. It's important; he'll understand," my dadima insisted. She then turned to my mother. "Eh, Shamim. Am I not right? Your brother would not mind for something this important, no?"

"No, Ma. It's best to wait until he's fresh," my father responded.

"*Haya.* Your choice. What do I know? I am just an old woman."

My mother placed a cup of tea in front of my dadima and a glass of milk in front of me. "How could this be, Shiraz? It makes no sense."

My father tapped a pencil to the table and shook his head.

"That is why I am saying call now," my dadima said, shuffling in her seat.

"Oh God, are you deaf or what? Didn't you hear your son? He said we'll wait until a decent hour." My mother stood against the kitchen counter, rubbing her arms over her red wool sweater.

"Am I saying something so vile? No. All I am saying is that we should get to the bottom of this right away. What is the point in waiting? Let's just find out the truth right now."

"What do you mean, truth?" my mother asked.

"Your brother will have all the answers, I am sure." My dadima ripped open a packet of Sweet'N Low and poured it into her teacup.

"Don't talk in riddles. Say what you want to say."

"Dear God, am I not allowed to ask even the simplest of questions in this house?"

My father slapped his hand to the table. "Okay enough! I don't want any fighting in this house. This is all some sort of mistake. An accounting error. We'll find out what happened to our money and that will be the end of it."

THAT EVENING we gathered around the phone as if it were a talisman. My father moved the phone from the living room to the kitchen table, the cord like a snake behind him. It took several tries before my father got through, and even then, the line was fuzzy.

"WHAT? YES, YES, CANADA IS VERY COLD."

...

"YES, EVERYONE IS FINE."

...

"LISTEN JIMMY, I DON'T HAVE MUCH TIME HERE." My father went on to explain the situation.

Jimmy Uncle was flabbergasted. He had never encountered any problems whatsoever with the bank himself. He then told him not to worry—he would get to the bottom of things. Guaranteed.

"WE NEED THE MONEY RIGHT AWAY, JIMMY. TO CLOSE THE DEAL. THERE'S NO TIME TO WASTE. "

Jimmy Uncle said that he would look into things immediately and report back as soon as he had any information at all.

Before my father hung up, my mother motioned for him to give her the phone.

"Be quick," my father said. "This is costing me a fortune."

My mother took the receiver from my father. She hurried her words, repeating several times. "PLEASE, JIMMY, JUST FIND OUR MONEY."

After my mother hung up, my father made my dadima promise not to tell the family back home. There was no need to worry them unnecessarily. We would find the money.

In the middle of the night, I woke up for a glass of water. A soft light illuminated the kitchen. The stove's hood light was on. I could hear the muffled sound of voices. I turned the corner to see my parents sitting at the kitchen table, their chairs facing each other, their knees pressed together. My father's face was in his hands, my mother's hands wrapped around his wrists. I quickly returned to my room and tried to fall asleep, my stomach in a knot of worry.

JIMMY UNCLE CALLED often, but each time, he did not have any news. These things take time, he said.

The Department of the Environment said that they could not wait any longer; they had many other interested applicants. My father's deal was cancelled.

A week later, it was decided that my mother should take a job. She searched for a job as a bookkeeper or as a secretary, something akin to her training, but at interviews she was told that she needed Canadian experience. She eventually found a job at a door and window factory, working the night shift, 6 p.m. to 4 a.m.

The city was now completely frozen and covered in snow. My mother wrapped her plants in layers of burlap; they looked like ghosts, sitting at the edge of the balcony. My dadima complained incessantly about the cold; she sat at the kitchen table bundled in several shawls and a toque. My mother refused to incur higher heating costs. "If you don't like the weather, just wait a few hours," she said to my dadima, echoing a saying in the city. And sure enough, days later a Chinook blew in, raising temperatures to above normal and filling the streets, and our balcony, with pools of melted snow. Overnight, my snow chart went from seven centimetres to zero.

On the first day that my mother went to work, it was evident that our life had changed. We ate as soon as I got home from school, and rushed through our dinner. My mother needed to leave the house by five o'clock. The factory was an hour away, on the outskirts of Calgary.

Soon, my mother started cooking simpler meals, some of which she had learned about from her co-workers, meals like shepherd's pie and meat loaf. On the days that she was exceptionally tired, she would serve frozen dinners. She had seen commercials on TV for products like Swanson TV Dinners, which promised a convenient and nutritious way for working women to feed their families. She asked my father to add TV dinners and other frozen items to the grocery list. To my dadima's dismay, my father had volunteered to do the grocery shopping. He and I would often spend hours at Safeway as he slowly pushed a shopping cart up and down the aisles, trying to find all the products on my mother's list.

Once, after my mother sped off to get dressed for work, my dadima hovered around my father as he and I cleared the table. It was strange for me to see my father doing housework. In Nairobi, we had servants, and here, my mother did all the cleaning. She had never asked me to do any chores, so helping out was new for me also.

"It's not proper, Shiraz," my dadima said, reaching for the plate in my father's hands. "Let me and the girl do it."

"*Na-na,* Ma. It's okay," my father said, raising the plate above her reach. "We can do it. You go watch TV."

My dadima refused to leave. She sat at the kitchen table. She spoke some English, but she only read Gujerati. She sat with one hand on her lap, the other flipping through my schoolbooks, licking her finger each time she turned the page of *Science Made Easy.*

My father brushed a heap of chewed chicken bones into the garbage and then filled the sink with hot water. I stood next to him on a step stool, ready to dry.

"I'm almost ready," my mother bellowed from the bathroom.

"The car will be warm in ten minutes." My father dropped the sponge into the sink, quickly wiped his hands on a dishtowel and rushed out.

I stood behind the balcony's glass doors and watched for my father. Soon, I saw him step out of his massive burgundy Impala. He banged a fist to the side-view mirror to push it back in place. Then he stood back and held the door open for my mother. I could see their breath billow and rise above them as they spoke.

"Of course let him get the car for *her*," my dadima mumbled from behind me in the kitchen. "But let *me* try asking. It will be my *murrow* only, the end of me. Ya Mowla, what, what have I done to deserve such a life, such ungrateful children? Please, I beg of you."

I turned to see her raise her eyes and palms to the ceiling, her *tasbih* dangling from the fingers of one hand. "Take me. Take me now. What are you waiting for?" she moaned.

Outside, my father bent down, stretching one arm over the hood. He leaned in and kissed my mother. He then closed the door and waited while she drove away, the car disappearing around the corner to McLeod Trail.

My father returned a few minutes later. We continued washing dishes.

My dadima wrapped her *tasbih* around her wrist. "What is the use of having a wife if you have to do all the dirty work, hanh? That is the problem, you see," she said, waving a finger to the air.

Her *tasbih* jangled against her gold bangles. "That woman has turned you into her wife. Don't say I didn't warn you."

"Be careful," my father said as he handed me a bowl that felt too big in my hands.

My dadima coughed. She flipped open Beatrix Potter's *Peter Rabbit.* "Why not go to London yourself? Find out what is happening, no?"

My father unplugged the sink drain. He shook his head. "Too expensive. Even the charters." My father lifted me off the stool. "Okay, time to say our *du'a.*" We walked to the living room, hand in hand, and waited for my grandmother to follow.

I said both *du'as,* and my father both *tasbihs.* I suggested that we also sing a *ginan.* I wanted to do something to cheer my father up.

"Not tonight, *mitu,* I have too much work. You watch some TV and then it's time for bed, okay?" He ruffled my hair and went back to the kitchen.

My dadima followed him.

I sat on the couch, doodling on my Etch-a-Sketch and then shaking it clean. I was fascinated by how quickly my drawings could disappear. On TV, the anchorman was talking about the Thriller in Manila, a boxing match between Joe Frazier and Muhammad Ali. It was the first event ever to be broadcast by satellite. Behind the anchor was an image of a satellite receiver; it looked like a giant ear with a probe pointed toward the sky. Ali had won after a long, gruelling battle. One sportswriter criticized

Ali for publicly belittling Frazier before the fight. They cut to a clip of Ali depicting Frazier as a gorilla. He then went on to call him an Uncle Tom, too dumb and ugly to be champion. He reminded me of some of my classmates at recess. After a few more reports, the weatherman appeared. I watched as a laced pattern of snowflakes decorated the map of Alberta.

"Snow! Daddy! It's going to snow again."

My father leaned back in his chair, holding himself steady with fingers curled under the table. He squinted at the TV. "Very good," he said.

"Can we go skiing this weekend? Please, Daddy?"

"We'll see, bheta. Right now, I have too much work."

After putting me to bed, my father took a shower. He used to shower in the morning, but now, since my mother had started working, he also showered at night. It was, he said, a good way to generate heat. Once, when I woke to go to the bathroom, he was still in the shower. As I waited outside in the hall, I thought I heard him call me.

"What, Daddy?"

He didn't respond.

I put my ear to the door. "What, Daddy?"

Still he didn't respond. That's when I realized he wasn't calling me. He was talking to himself. Suddenly, I felt an overwhelming pity for him. It both shocked and terrified me. I imagined my father shrinking inside the steaming shower. I wanted to pull open the door and let in some fresh air. Instead, I went back to my room. Under the nightlight, I examined the framed picture of my parents at Mount Kilimanjaro. In the picture, my parents are holding hands and my father is pointing to Kibo, the tallest cone, where, he once told me, there is a dormant volcano that still emits steam and sulfur. "But you never know," my father had said, "when it might erupt again." I hung my *tasbih* around the picture frame like a garland and then lay down and tried to sleep.

"Look, daddy!" I said, rushing in from the balcony, my finger at the eleven-centimetre mark on our snow-ruler. "We can go skiing this weekend for sure. Right?"

"Don't bother your father. He's trying to eat," my mother said. She stood at the stove, one arm on her hip as she fried *puris,* small bubbles forming at the top of each doughy circle. "Besides, it's too much money."

"Who said anything about money?" my father asked, shaking his head. "We'll go, *mitu.* Most definitely. Maybe not this weekend. But soon. It's not a matter of money, but time." He leaned forward and cupped my chin in his palm. "You understand, no?"

"Uh-huh."

"Call your dadima," my mother instructed, throwing a dish-towel over her shoulder. "Dinner's ready."

My dadima was in the living room watching *Stampede Wrestling.* I went to call her and then returned to clear my books off the kitchen table.

My dadima shuffled in, her *tasbih* dangling from her fingers. She sat down next to my father, who was busy opening the mail.

"Farah, go turn off the TV. So much waste," my mother said, releasing the oven door; it slammed shut, shaking the pots on the stovetop.

I returned to the kitchen and sat down at the table. My mother slid a Swanson Salisbury steak TV dinner, steam rising from the rice pudding, in front of my father, then my dadima, then me, and finally herself.

My dadima reached for a bottle of red chili powder and vigorously shook it over each tinfoil compartment, even the rice pudding. She sighed heavily.

My mother pounded a fistful of forks and knives onto the table. "No one said you have to eat it."

"Then what am I supposed to eat, hanh? Nothing?" She turned to my father. "You see that, Shiraz." My dadima wagged a finger in the air. "Your wife is trying to kill me only. Wants me to starve to death."

"Oh-ho," my father interrupted, a forkful of peas near his mouth. "Can't we just eat in peace?"

My mother pulled back her chair and sat down.

We ate silently. The clinking of our forks and knives echoed through the apartment. My dadima was unaccustomed to cutlery; she picked up the steak with her hands, planted her elbows on the table, and nibbled at it. Soon, she slapped it down.

"Let me get you something else," my father offered. "Kentucky *khupey?* You like their chicken."

"No, bheta, I'm fine," she said, and pulled a finger through the rice pudding, creating a tunnel.

"It won't take me long."

"Why are you spoiling her?" my mother asked as she carved a piece of steak. "If she doesn't want to eat it, let her be. Money doesn't grow on trees."

"You want money, hanh?" My dadima reached down into her maxi and retrieved a bundle of shillings, held together with an elastic band. She waved the money at my mother. "Take it! Take it if you think I am such a burden."

My mother clucked her tongue and then turned her head toward me. "See that? Your dadima—I swear she's mad. As if we don't have enough things to worry about."

"Stop it," my father said firmly. "Stop this nonsense."

My dadima continued. "If it wasn't for your thieving brother, we wouldn't have anything to worry about. *Haramjada!* Enjoying himself while we're here suffering like nobody's business."

"Suffering? Who's suffering? Not you, that's for sure. It's me breaking my back each and every day...."

"Stop it, Shamim," my father pleaded.

"No! Let her hear the truth for once. I'm sick and tired of all her nonsense. Doesn't lift a finger all day and still has the gall to complain. No wonder no one can stand living with her. Not even your father could take it anymore."

"Shamim!" My father banged his fork and knife down on the table.

"It's true!" My mother slapped the table. "Why are you trying to protect her?" she said angrily, and then turned to my dadima. It was as if she were a skier who had suddenly found herself on a dangerous run, but continued down it anyway, unable to stop herself. "Did you hear that, Ma? I said your husband couldn't take it anymore. He isn't dead! He left you. Even has a new wife. And who the hell can blame him?" My mother turned her gaze back to my father, her face flushed red. "Why don't *you* tell her, Shiraz? Go ahead. Tell her the truth for once in your life!"

In a single moment, my father stood up and reached across the table, his arm raised above him. But then, as if he were a machine that had stalled, his fist dropped down and smashed the table, making the plates and cutlery reverberate.

My father placed a palm to the table and then leaned in to my mother, pointing a finger at her face. "You want to hear the truth? The truth is that *your* brother stole our money," he said in a fierce tone. "And if it wasn't for him—that bastard—I would never be in this position. Never!" He threw his chair to the floor and stormed out. A few seconds later, a door slammed.

I sat at the table, terrified. It was as if I were inside a snow globe, which had been picked up and shaken ruthlessly; each part of me had unhinged itself from my body and now banged against the glass. I started to cry uncontrollably.

My mother, it seemed, was unable to move. She just stared at the table, the tips of her fingers over her lips.

My dadima dusted her hands over her TV dinner, wiped her mouth with a tea towel, and then lifted herself out of her chair. She shuffled away to our room, closing the door behind her.

THAT NIGHT my father slept on the couch. He lay still under a blanket, his arm over his eyes. I went to him and nudged him gently.

"Are you okay, *mituri?*" he asked, turning to me.

"Can I sleep here?"

He pushed himself against the back of the couch and pulled me in. "It's all going to be all right," he said, kissing my forehead.

I nodded, but in the street-light streaming into the living room, I could see his eyes were red. I pressed myself to him; his heart pounded against my back. Through the balcony's glass doors, I could see that it was snowing.

JIMMY UNCLE NEVER FOUND our money and we never found out what happened to it. My mother suggested we ask him to help us out. After everything my father had done for him, it was his duty. My father agreed on one condition: Jimmy Uncle had to accept responsibility for what had happened. But Jimmy Uncle refused. "Why should I?" he said. "Please, Jimmy. Please," my mother begged him. "But it wasn't my fault," he said. "Then whose fault was it?" my father asked my mother. In the end, my father took the money grudgingly. Jimmy Uncle could not replace all of it. Instead he sent a monthly stipend for years, which would on its arrival sometimes start an argument like a sudden snowstorm between my parents.

Eventually my father saved enough money to successfully apply for another government licence, this time for a Lottery Booth in Grande Prairie, far from the Rockies. My father, with my mother's help, grew the business to three lottery booths, two here in Grande Prairie and one in Peace River. In time, my father began sponsoring the rest of his family. My dadima lived with Kamru Uncle at first, but she was later admitted to a full-care nursing home, where she lives today. My aunties and uncles blamed my mother for the deterioration in her health.

My parents are now separated. My mother waited until I moved away for university before she finally left my father. "Who needs this bullshit?" she said to me. It was the first time I heard her swear in English. My mother lives in a condominium, a few blocks from my father. My father lives in the house I grew up in, a semi-detached bungalow on Hillcrest Drive. He and I never learned how to ski, although he still exercises each morning, speed walking the corridors of Grande Prairie's shopping malls.

I am now enrolled in Business School at the University of Alberta in Edmonton; I hope one day to be a chartered accountant. My father calls me almost every day. We often talk about the same things—the weather, what we had for dinner, our health. He mails me articles with titles like, "How to Avoid Lightning," "You and Your Heart," "Carbon Monoxide Detector Saves Family." The letters arrive, unmarked, a photocopy of the article inside. When I return to Grande Prairie during school breaks, I work at the Lottery Booth—just as I did when I was growing up. My father and I sit behind the counter, drinking Tim Hortons coffee or eating our lunch or dinner from one of the stalls in the food court. Many of my father's regular customers stop by daily even if they have already purchased their week's tickets. They are like friends now. They know him as Sam.

The Rubbermaid Princess

Zera Pirmohamed waves goodbye to Altaf as he drives toward the staff parking lot in his polished red Mustang, fitted with a car bra and spoilers. It is six-thirty in the morning, but the August sun still hasn't risen—stuck, it seems, under the Calgary horizon. *What would I do without him?* Zera thinks to herself as she steps through the revolving door of the Ralph Klein Auxiliary Hospital. Altaf is part of the Ismailia Volunteer Corps; he is responsible for driving the northeast jamati minibus, which takes seniors from areas like Whitehorn and Temple to jamatkhana for their morning prayers. Zera wishes she could attend jamatkhana, if only once in a while, but she has not been for years now. Zera relies on Altaf for other reasons. He helps her with her home-based cooking business, but more importantly, he works at the hospital's laundering facility on the early shift, 7 A.M. to 3 P.M., and gives Zera a ride to and from the hospital, allowing her to visit her son, Tajdin, more easily. Sixteen years ago, at age twenty-nine, Tajdin was in a terrible car accident and is still in a coma.

Inside the hospital, Zera first stops at The Gift Shop, as she does every morning, to purchase a copy of the *Calgary Herald.* She tucks the Saturday paper, which is packed with advertisement supplements, into her large canvas handbag. The handbag bears a screen-printed picture of a cowboy, his knee pushed into the back of a heifer that's been wrestled to the ground, his gloved hand wrapped around the rope that binds her legs together, and his arm triumphantly above him. The words across the top read: THE CALGARY STAMPEDE, THE GREATEST OUTDOOR SHOW ON EARTH. The volunteer salesclerk, in her candy-striped pinafore, smiles broadly as she gives Zera her change. Zera counts it carefully before she shovels it into a small gold-coloured change purse and tucks it down the front of her paisley print maxi. She turns to leave, oblivious to the clerk's giggles, and as she walks away, she rocks from side to side like the pendulum of a clock. Zera has arthritis in her hips and knees.

Zera continues, as she always does, down the long hallway directly to the elevator. These days, she is no longer aware of the acute smell of the hospital—as if pails of rotten eggs mixed with antiseptic have been used to sanitize the dull-white floors—a smell that used to make her pinch her nose. As the elevator doors open and close on the way up, Zera also doesn't see the patients wheeling oxygen tanks or IV bags with tubing trailing behind like overcooked noodles, or the ones in the dimly lit TV room, some of whom are sprawled out, ready for a long day, others with nurses bent over them, spoon-feeding them porridge or Jell-O. Instead she passes them as if she's riding a freight elevator in a warehouse. When an automated voice calls out, *"Floor Five— Cafeteria,"* Zera carefully steps off. Visiting hours in Tajdin's ward do not begin until eight o'clock.

Zera spends the first hour and a half in the cafeteria, where she orders her usual: a cup of hot water. She takes her cup to a table by a window that faces Suncrest Mall and sits down. The streets are empty today as they are on most weekend mornings. People are still at home, sleeping in, exhausted perhaps from the rigour of their week. Zera removes three Rubbermaid containers from her handbag—one stuffed with bags of Red Rose tea, another with a row of Maria biscuits. The last one is empty. She struggles to open them, her fingers still stiff from hours of cooking earlier this morning.

ZERA PATS A KITCHEN TOWEL to her sagging bosom and tries to soak up the oil that has spattered onto her cotton nightgown. She flips the towel over her shoulder, dips a wooden spoon into the simmering pot, and leaning over the stove, takes one final taste of the *kuku paka*. She shakes her head, reaches for the bottle of lemon juice, and pours generously. Pushing her thumb up against her teeth, she shifts her dentures back into place, then takes another taste. Yes, much better. Hopefully, even the fussy ones will like it very much. Some people, they just expect too much from the world. Sometimes in life, you have to compromise, accept things, instead of asking for so much. Yet, Zera has noticed, those who ask for a lot often get a lot—even if they do not deserve such a good life. Zera glances at the cluster of framed photographs of Tajdin on top of the microwave, which is speckled with grease. What, dear God, did he do to deserve such a fate? She tightens her grip around her wooden spoon. If only he had left his girlfriend's house a few minutes sooner.

A set of alarm clocks sits on the kitchen windowsill—one in the shape of the Prophet's mausoleum, another, a plaque with a poem about struggle as the meaning of life, a canary-yellow one with bluebirds that was Tajdin's as a child, and an electric one with number-cards that flip forward. The Prophet's mausoleum rings; Zera slaps it shut. It's already 2:15 in the morning; Altaf will be here soon. She rushes to the pantry, which is stacked from floor to ceiling with Rubbermaid containers in all shapes and colours. She removes several sets and lines them up according to size, first covering the kitchen counter, then the dining table, and finally, bending slowly, she resorts to the floor. Smells of coconut and coriander rise from the *kuku paka* as she shuffles to the counter, carrying the heavy pot. She carefully sets the pot down and wipes her sleeve across her nose. She then ladles the right amount of sauce, chicken, and eggs into the different containers. Many of her customers order only for big occasions like Eid or when relatives were coming, but some families are on a daily schedule—mostly the youths, who nowadays, thank God, hire people to do everything in their houses: cooking, cleaning, mowing, shovelling, fixing-bixing. Just like back home in Tanzania, Zera thinks. But who knew that one day she would be the servant?

Soon after they arrived in Canada in 1975, Tajdin's father died quietly in his sleep, leaving Zera a widow at the age of forty-five. The doctor had not been able to say what happened. "He seemed in good health," he said, "especially for a seventy-year-old." Zera was sure that her husband's body had just given up—unable to adjust to all the changes of moving to a new country. Men's bodies are like that—the slightest of problems, a little cold, an upset stomach, an ache here or there, and *kalas*. All day they will be complaining like a *kasuku*. And who wants to listen to a parrot all day? But women's bodies, now *they* are very different. Built to endure pain. Otherwise how else would we be able to survive childbirth? Mind you, Zera had not experienced childbirth herself.

Tajdin was only twenty-three when his father died; still, he told Zera confidently, "Don't worry, Mummy. I'll take care of everything." He was at SAIT studying Hotel and Restaurant Management. Until he graduated and was able to work full-time, Tajdin took up various part-time jobs, like the one at Superstore where he wore roller skates and helped customers quickly locate items among its vast aisles. After paying off his student loans, he had saved enough for a down payment on a house, and they moved out of their basement suite in Pembrooke to a nicer area of town. "What blessings to have such a good son," Zera told the neighbours. "Finally, we will be able to move to a proper house!" They had been living in their Falconridge townhouse for a year when Tajdin had the car accident.

Zera now turns off the stove's whirring hood fan and sprays a little Joy perfume into a bowl that is made out of tinfoil and lined with sugar. She places the bowl on the front element of the stove, hoping to fumigate the house. This is yet another reason she doesn't like cooking. All the smells that seep into her walls and, like stubborn stains, are impossible to remove. Zera often wishes she hadn't been forced to close down her fourteen-year-old house-cleaning business—a business she opened after Tajdin had been in a coma for three months. Her body had ached with pain after a day's work, but cleaning gave her great satisfaction. Cleaning was nothing like cooking: the evidence of your hard work did not disappear in minutes. You could admire your work all day—in the shining sink, the gleaming floors, the perfectly tucked-in sheets, or the stacks of neatly folded towels. If only the extra-strength Tylenol and hot-water bottles still worked for her. Two years ago, she found she could no longer bend over bathtubs, carry vacuum cleaners up and down the stairs of those big-big houses, or scrub the floors to the same shine. Business dwindled even when she cut her rates in half and placed weekly flyers—like so many others: Tammy's Aesthetics & Hair Salon—Best

Prices in Town, Amyn's Auto: Lube & Oil Change Special, Amway, A Sure Way to Success!—under the windshields of the cars parked outside Calgary's jamatkhanas.

Zera fills the other rows of containers with rice, *faloodho,* and chutney. She lets the steam escape, then snaps the lids on, running her finger around the outer edge to make sure each one is tightly sealed. She pulls a sheet of plastic wrap from a restaurant-sized roll, purchased at Costco, and wraps it over a stack of *manis.* She then places each completed order in a plastic Safeway bag that has been pre-labelled with the customer's name using masking tape and a red marker. She is about to go to her room and get ready when Altaf raps lightly on the glass patio door. Zera looks up in surprise. She checks her many clocks: 2:45 A.M. Why is he early?

At the beginning, Zera asked people to pick up their tiffins, but then she heard that Roshan Dossa's husband died of a heart attack as he shovelled the walk after a heavy snowstorm, and she was now offering a delivery service with her tiffins. Zera started to deliver to as many customers as she could—she knew the bus routes well. One day on his way to work, Altaf saw her at a bus stop and stopped to offer her a ride. He suggested that he could help her regularly. She said no at first, but eventually accepted when he agreed to take money and a daily lunch tiffin. She did not want to carry any *bhar,* the weight of returning a favour. Now, they had a well-established routine. Each day he arrived at three in the morning. Zera would accompany him as he picked up the seniors, then dropped them off to jamatkhana, after which he and Zera would make their rounds to her customers—most of whom lived in areas like Coral Springs with its man-made lakes or Edgemont with its perfect vistas of the Rocky Mountains. From some of those houses, the specially built ski-jumps at Canada Olympic Park were clearly visible, like gigantic cement waterfalls in the middle of the valley. What a waste, Zera thought. So much money just so a few people could jump from here to there. I swear, people who have nothing to worry about always spend their money foolishly. When they arrived at a customer's house, Zera would sit in the minibus while Altaf tied the plastic bags around the doorknobs of front doors or left them in designated spots like a children's swing set in the backyard. Altaf had mapped out an efficient route and their timing never varied. Calgary's roads were consistently empty at this hour, so Altaf joked to Zera, "Who needs to go to jamatkhana when you can meditate right here on McKnight Boulevard?" They would return to jamatkhana in time for the driver making the return trip at six o'clock and then transfer into Altaf's Mustang for the drive to the hospital.

Zera rushes to meet Altaf at the patio door. Did one of her alarms not go off? What if I've upset him—then what? She partially slides open the door. "Sorry, bheta, sorry. I didn't know I was running late ..."

"*Ya Ali Madat,* Ma." Altaf rubs his goatee, shaved in the style of a Zanzibari man. (And to think he's from Uganda!) Altaf is tall and plump; his belly presses against his pullover and makes him look like a man of more experience than his thirty-one years. He adjusts his gold-rimmed glasses. "I couldn't sleep, so I thought I'd come and see if you needed a hand."

"So nice of you. But everything is fine, bheta." Why hadn't he called first? "I'm sorry, I'm not even ready yet."

"*Aye-wino*. Take your time. I'll wait."

Everything inside Zera falls into disarray—as if a completed puzzle had been turned upside down, the pieces scattered on the ground. Oh God, what choice did she have now? "Come, bheta, come. Have some tea and *tepala* first."

"No, don't worry. You go and get ready. I'll start loading the minibus."

"Sure? It won't take long at all."

"Seriously, Ma. *Bhook-nye-laygee.*"

Altaf, like so many youngsters these days, mixed-up English, Kutchi, and Swahili—as if they were cooking *kichro,* Zera thought. Why couldn't they speak one or the other properly, like the British, instead of this Canadian-style English, mumble-jumbling everything from anywhere and everywhere they liked? Zera's father had insisted that she and her brothers, as well as their mother, take turns reading the English newspaper to him. "This is the way of the new world," he would say and point to a photograph of the Imam with his beautiful European wife. Under the photo was the inscription *"Adopt simple colonial dress. Yours affectionately, Aga Khan."* Zera's father would lie on his *charphoy* while the reader stood at full attention next to him and another sibling massaged his feet. One error in pronunciation and *kalas*—he would dispense a slap across the poor reader's face. Try crying and you'd only get another. But worse than the double slap was the fear generated for the foot masseur. The slap would often create an equal and opposite reaction, as in a line of dominoes, somewhere else in their father's body. If you were lucky, he would only release a loud rumbling fart, but if not, then the poor masseur would get a swift kick out of nowhere.

Zera sighs in relief at Altaf's refusal for tea. "Okay, bheta. Your choice. But I'm telling you, you have to eat properly, otherwise you'll shrink up into nothing."

"I'm fine, can't you see?" Altaf smiles as he rubs his belly.

"What you talking? You're too skinny. Maybe your Farzu has you wrapped around her finger, hanh?" Zera teases. Altaf is getting married next year to his long-time girlfriend, Farzana Visram, who is adamant that he get into shape before the wedding.

"Maybe, Ma, maybe. But she's a modern woman—what can I do? You know how they are. Men—we're fools in love and still, it's always the women who complain! I tell you, I should have had my bride shipped over from Bombay, huh?" He winks, then laughs.

Zera just smiles, but inside she feels the weight of her heart, like a stone, as her mind travels back to India and Fateh. The afternoon sun was strong and most people were inside resting.

Zera stood with her foot against the back wall of their house, one hand in her pants pocket, the other gently wiggling her loose tooth. Zera had four older brothers and despite her mother's protests, she insisted on wearing what they did—pants, shirts, pyjamas, even boys' underwear. Zera never much liked dresses—the way they billowed up and made her feel as if she might float away. She liked the feel of cloth against her legs—the way pants shaped her body and allowed her to take long confident strides. Zera was eager for her tooth to fall out and be replaced with a permanent tooth, but the wiggling—this ability to create a sensation in her body simply by moving one part if it—felt so good that she wanted to savour it. The tooth persistently hung on, prompting Fateh Khoja, the neighbour's son, his yellow kite trailing on the ground behind him like a snake in the grass, to tease her. "What you so scared about? Just pull it out, stupid girl."

All the boys liked Fateh. He was the champion of all kite-flying competitions in Mandvi. He had even won a prize at Ahmedabad's Uttarayan, the Hindu festival celebrating the awakening of the gods from winter's deep slumber. Fateh's kites boasted the best designs, favouring intricate geometric shapes painted in the brightest pinks, yellows, and oranges. Boys often stood on rooftops challenging each other to kite-fights, their lines coated with ground glass. Fateh manoeuvred his kite with such skill that he was able to cut his opponent's line and bring it falling to the ground in a matter of seconds. Zera didn't like him one little bit. He was always bothering her whenever he got a chance.

"Go to hell," Zera said loudly and clearly. "I can do anything I want."

Fateh yanked his kite forward. "Pull it, I said! Otherwise I'll do it for you."

It was as if Fateh had pressed a lever and released a spring in Zera's body. Her hand shot out and punched him. Fateh cupped his mouth. Zera stepped back. He was older and stronger and her first instinct was to run, but something inside made her stand firm. She clenched her fists and looked directly at him. Yes! She would pummel the idiot another if that's what was required. Fateh slammed his hands flat against the wall and trapped her between his arms. He leaned his face toward hers.

"Arrey." He smiled as blood trickled down the side of his mouth. "Who knew you were such a clever girl, hanh?"

Zera looked away. She felt like cut glass as she stood against the wall, the hot sunshine pouring through her.

Fateh winked, and as he walked away, he turned back briefly. "You wait and see, Zera Pirmohamed. I'm going to marry you one day."

The next day Zera found Fateh on the roof of the building, his yellow kite with its long tail soaring above him. She marched up to him and tugged the kite string, which had been chalked with pink dust, as if she were pulling a bell. When Fateh turned to her, she whirled around and marched a few steps away before lying down on the hot roof, her mouth wide open. Fateh went to her and straddled her like a wishbone. Zera's eyes followed his kite, which flapped under the sky, as Fateh leaned down, wound his kite string tightly around her tooth and pulled it with one flick of his wrist. A few drops of blood trickled down to the back of her throat. She swallowed. Then tongued the socket, but quickly recoiled. It was too sensitive. She stood up and wiped her mouth with her palm, leaving a smudge of pink chalk across her lips and fingers. She then dusted off her pants. "Thank you," she said to her future husband as he placed the tooth in her open palm. Zera climbed down the makeshift ladder, and at home she stored her tooth safely inside an empty perfume tin the size of her ring finger.

Soon Zera and Fateh became inseparable; many people even referred to them as one person. Fateh–Zera spent countless days pretending to be Kutchi pirates plundering the treasures of royal sea vessels, pretending sword fights between the Mughal army and the Ghurkhas, or building elaborate sandcastles.

Once, Zera arrived on the beach to find Fateh wearing a peacock-blue paper crown made from one of his kites. Behind him—a mound of sand covered by a shirt. "What is that?" she asked, smiling. He snapped off the shirt like a magician to reveal a lopsided replica of the Taj Mahal, complete with a garden made of jasmine petals and a seawater pond. "Not bad," Zera said as she leaned in for a closer look. "But I could build a better one."

"Highly unlikely," Fateh countered, and before she could say anything, he presented her with a bright pink paper crown.

Zera tried not to shake when he placed it on her head.

"I now pronounce you princess of my castle."

"But the one that Emperor Shah Jehan built for Mumtaz Mahal is made of white marble and filled with gems," Zera teased, and turned to run, certain Fateh would chase her.

Instead, he just wagged his finger at her and laughed. "Silly girl, you'll eat your words when I build a Taj filled with more rubies and diamonds than any emperor could afford for his wife."

No one objected to Zera and Fateh's friendship and over the years, their affection for each other continued to grow deeper. Their families were long-time friends and welcomed the idea. In fact, when Fateh's father sent him, at the age of eighteen, like so many other young Kutchi and Gujerati boys before, to build fortunes in Zanzibar and help the family escape their impoverished lives, it was taken for granted that Fateh would, in good time, send for Zera. She was fifteen and would soon be of marriageable age. For the first year, Fateh sent regular correspondence, but then the letters—delivered by young men returning not only with tales of their grand lives on the dark continent but also to fetch their new wives—came to a full stop. Zera's family enquired about Fateh's whereabouts and asked for the wedding date to be fixed, but Fateh's father was vague and said he too hadn't heard anything for quite some time.

Zera did not give up hope and refused to entertain the many marriage proposals she received—threatening to kill herself if her father forced her. Instead, she spent hours at the harbour, staring out at the vastness of the Arabian Sea. She stood on her tiptoes and imagined seeing, out over the undulating waves, the tip of Arabia, the coast of Africa, the edge of Zanzibar. Each time a steamer appeared in the distance, she would jump up. "He's come! Finally, he's come." Sailors soon became accustomed to seeing her when they arrived at Mandvi port. Word about Zera's antics spread for miles and she received fewer and fewer marriage proposals. "*Hai-Ram!* Have you heard about that one? Gone completely mad. Poor thing! Lost her chance now. Already twenty-two."

One proposal trickled in later that year, and to her parents' delight, Zera accepted. The bridegroom was a forty-seven-year-old widower who had returned from Zanzibar after his wife died in childbirth; he was in search of a new wife to take care of him and his new child. Each night, on the steamer to Africa, Zera resisted her husband's advances—secretly shoving a finger down her throat to feign seasickness. Her husband left her alone, told her he was in no hurry. As the steamer sailed closer to Zanzibar, Zera lay awake at night next to her new husband and made more and more intricate plans about the perfect life she would lead with her *real* husband.

The steamer arrived in Stone Town the same day Princess Elizabeth was crowned Queen of England. As passengers disembarked, fezzed officers from the King's African Rifles handed them tins of Cadbury's chocolate decorated with the royal insignia. When Zera went to Fateh's shop, he told her that he was very glad to see her, but he only laughed when she told him her plans. "Eh-ma! But I am already married with children. I am sorry for your trouble—I did not mean any harm. But what we had was only child's play, no?"

Zera was so stunned that she could not will her body to move or form thoughts into words; it was as if she were trapped in the terror of a dream where she was trying to run away from a monster but her feet were cemented to the ground and her screams were silent. Zera stood in front of Fateh like a statue, waiting for him to take her in his arms and wake her.

Fateh led her to the door and sent her home.

Zera returned, in a daze, to her new husband's house, where he rushed to her and handed her the baby. "What's a good boy's name?" he asked. He said he hadn't had the heart to name the child after his wife died. Zera named him Tajdin and made him hers. All the years they were married, Zera refused to open herself to her new husband and he never pressured her to consummate their marriage.

Now an alarm goes off. Three o'clock. "Oh-ho, let me rush," Zera says to Altaf.

Altaf removes his shoes and enters the kitchen, walking to the row of blue recycling bins, which are filled with the tiffins. "*Haya,* I'll be in the bus."

Zera hurries to the bathroom to get dressed. She quickly combs her short thin hair, dips a finger into a large tub of pink hair gel before applying it to her hairline to fix it in place. She used to use Yardley's, but Tajdin said it made her smell like a man;

he suggested that she try his Dep. He also suggested she wear maxis like so many other women her age, instead of her pantsuits. Zera fishes out a long gold chain from a small dish on top of the toilet tank, and slips it around her neck, tucking the excess into her maxi. She then reaches for her ivory cable-knit sweater, which hangs on a white plastic hook behind the door. A crumpled-up tissue falls out of a sleeve. The sweater used to fit her properly but over the years it has stretched, and now hangs well past her ample hips. Zera struggles with the buttons and finally, when she's done, she turns a bottle of Avon perfume (one of the many gifts Tajdin bought her for Mother's Day after they learned about the holiday in Canada) upside down against her fingertip, then daubs it at the base of her neck and behind her ears. She shoves her small gold-coloured change purse into her bra, wraps her *tasbih* around her wrist, and walks to the back door, where she slips her feet into dull-white running shoes with Velcro straps for laces. The sole of her right shoe has partially separated at the heel and sometimes gapes open like the mouth of a scared child.

Zera steps out into the cool August morning. The stars look blue against the dark sky and the silence at this time of the day makes her feel as if she's placed her ear to a seashell—all she can hear is a hollow echo. She locks the patio door and walks carefully along the gravel path through the unkempt backyard; the lawn is patched with brown grass and the branches on the shrubs are folded over, touching the ground, as if in exhaustion. Altaf has offered to help with the garden, but Zera refused. How much could she expect one person to do? Zera pushes open the back gate to the alley where Altaf has parked the minibus.

THE CAFETERIA BEGINS to fill with the regulars as Zera squeezes the teabag over her cup and then places it in the empty Rubbermaid container. She puts two Maria cookies on the table, then snaps the lids of all three containers closed before tucking them into her handbag. Zera turns to see the morning-shift nurses from Tajdin's floor in the cafeteria lineup. One smiles and waves. Zera nods hello, then looks outside, leaning over her cup to take a bite of her tea-soaked cookie; she watches a lone car obediently stop when the traffic light turns from green to yellow to red. From the very beginning, Zera has never liked many of the nurses. They do not attend to Tajdin in a prompt manner; instead, they spend their time in idle chit-chat at the nurses' station—discussing, Zera is sure, how to get one of the doctors to marry them. (But what doctor would marry those lazy *hoonts?*)

Zera was about to report them to the hospital administration, when she received a letter asking her to see the hospital's attorney. The doctors had conducted new tests and they wanted her to know that they would fully support the family's decision to remove life support. This way, the attorney had said, she would also be able to access Tajdin's bank accounts. When Zera didn't answer, he asked her if she'd like a translator—they had several Indian doctors on staff and he didn't mind checking to see if one was on duty. Zera pressed her hands against the armrests of her chair, pushed herself up, and walked out of his office.

That week, she started collecting samples from Tajdin: nail clippings, tufts of hair (head and chest, especially over the heart), and stool samples. She stored them in a set of colour-coded Rubbermaid containers. Altaf confirmed, through a friend at the hospital's medical laboratory, that there was nothing at all to worry about. Tajdin was alive. Zera continues to collect samples regularly—each month on Chandraat, after *mukhi-sahib* has performed the *chanta* ceremony, gently spraying Tajdin's face with holy water to forgive his sins and bid him a speedy recovery.

Zera quickly finishes her biscuits, stands and slowly weaves between the cafeteria tables, choosing a route that avoids the nurses, and heads toward the elevators.

Every few months Tajdin shares a room with a new patient. The current one: a man who has had several strokes that have left one side of his body paralyzed. The man, like many previous patients, doesn't receive many visitors and is eager to share his story with anyone he can. Each time, Zera would just shake her head, wave her hand at them, and say, "No speak the English," before she pulled the dividing curtain, which also, thankfully, shut out the persistent prairie sun that spilled in through the room's two small windows, even during the coldest winter days.

Zera squeezes Tajdin's cheek as she would a tomato for ripeness. "*Ya Ali Madat,* bheta. How's it? Everything okay?" Zera admires her son—such a good-looking boy. Lost some weight over the years because of those useless nurses, but his face is still nice and round. And nothing can take away his fair-fair skin. Zera proudly remembers neighbours joking with her, "Sure he wasn't switched at birth?" Tajdin was easily mistaken for a European or at least an Arab—especially with his light grey eyes—eyes that sometimes, still, out of nowhere, pop open as if he is waking from a bad dream or waking because he has suddenly remembered something that he has to tell his mother. The first few times, Zera ecstatically pressed the call button over and over again, but when the nurse finally arrived she said it was important not to get overly excited. The nurse went on to explain that it was a natural reflex, like going to the bathroom, and it didn't mean anything. "Your son," she said, "is still in a sleep state and isn't aware of his surroundings." Now, when Tajdin opens his eyes, Zera runs her palm over them to close them. No point in the boy straining his eye muscles.

Zera adjusts the respirator tube around Tajdin's chin and nose, then reaches behind him for a light switch. The wall lamp flickers briefly before expiring. Ah! Zera checks the side table to see if there are any light bulbs stored in the drawer, and when she finds none, she cracks open the door to the washroom behind her and turns the timer for the light to its maximum, thirty minutes. She drags a chair closer to his bed and removes the *Calgary Herald* from her canvas bag. There is a thick stack of flyers in the centre-fold, but a few are also hidden between the sections. She separates the paper and, as she flips through, without meaning to, she starts to read out the various headlines: SCIENTISTS WARN OF SEVERE CLIMATE CHANGE ... WOMAN DIES NEAR RESERVE ... ISRAEL IMPOSES STRICT CLOSURES IN THE WEST BANK AND GAZA STRIP ... 14 DIE IN SUICIDE BOMBING ... REFORM REPLACES BLOC AS OFFICIAL OPPOSITION ... POLICY OF "CONTAINMENT" OF SADDAM HUSSEIN SLOWLY ERODING ... SCHOOL BUS COLLISION NEAR AIRDRIE: 17 DEAD. Zera catches herself and stops: she had forgotten that she no longer reads the newspaper. Zera does not want to fill Tajdin's ears with the constant disappointment of the world. She clears her throat and starts to read the advertisements to him, making sure she enunciates each word clearly. MARK'S WORK WEARHOUSE: BACK TO SCHOOL EXTRAVAGANZA! ... STOCK UP AND SAVE AT DOLLAR-MART ... THE BRICK: BUY NOW AND DON'T PAY UNTIL 1998 ... The timer for the light switch wheezes softly like a distant snore, and then the light goes out.

Zera folds the newspaper and, before tucking it into her handbag, roots through to retrieve her Walkman. Tajdin had given her his old Walkman after he bought a newer model. She used to carry it on evening digestion walks around their townhouse complex. Tajdin had also encouraged her to use it when he invited his friends around to watch *Hockey Night in Canada, Monday Night Football,* The PGA Tour, and other sporting events on the satellite TV he had purchased. Zera would sit in her bedroom with her headphones on (in case Tajdin came in to see how she was doing), but she would not play her *ginan* tapes. She preferred listening to the boys' voices filling the house with laughter and screams of glee when one of their favourite teams scored.

Tajdin had been an avid sportsman himself. Always voted best player at everything—traditional volleyball at The Ismaili Triangular Games, Ismaili Ball Hockey League, Ismaili Student Association Bowl-a-rama, Ismaili Youth Camp Soccer League— you name it, he was the champion. No wonder his friends called him Touchdown Taj. (They even had it inscribed on a T-shirt for him. That is how much reverence they had for the boy!) No wonder all the girls followed him like fools, even if Salma had been his girlfriend for so many years. Should have broken it off with that girl! I knew it only. Wish I had said something when I had a chance. What good was she? Hadn't that hussy gone off with someone new only months after Tajdin's accident? No shame at all—the youth these days. Can't wait for anything. Everything has to be fast-fast: fast food, fast money, fast love. That is their problem.

But then a thought occurs to Zera: What has years of waiting done for me? Her hands tremble as she quickly slips the headphones on and firmly pushes down the play button. Nothing happens. She taps the Walkman against the edge of chair. She isn't sure if the tape she always listens to, *Ginan-e-Sharif,* is now too old, or if the Walkman is worn out. She ejects the tape and cleans it with the edge of her maxi before she reinserts it. Abida Parveen's beautiful voice starts to croon in her ear, and for the next hour, Zera's head bobs back and forth, side to side, as she drifts in and out of sleep.

Zera spends most of the day like this, then wakes to have her lunch—a rolled-up piece of *mani* sprinkled with sugar and a cup of tea—dozes again, wakes when a nurse pulls open the dividing curtain and comes in to clean Tajdin's bedpan, dozes and wakes until her Timex sports watch, another gift from her son, buzzes intermittently and she packs her things, kisses her son goodbye, telling him what's on the menu tomorrow (*ghos-jo-saag,* rice, and *kheer*), and then rushes to the front entrance where she waits for Altaf. After this morning's fiasco, she doesn't want to keep him waiting again. She stands inside and watches carefully for his approaching car. Twenty minutes later, Altaf arrives at the regular time, 3:15 P.M., and drives her home.

Altaf pulls into Zera's townhouse complex: a maze of tall slim houses, painted in alternating rows of dark brown with light-brown trim and light brown with dark-brown trim. Children scatter and women push their strollers aside as Altaf winds his way around the narrow inner road to Zera's house.

"Thank you, bheta," Zera says, and slips his empty lunch tiffin into her handbag. "Don't come early tomorrow. You sleep properly, okay?" Zera inches herself out of Altaf's car, places her handbag on the ground, and then, using the frame of the door for support, pushes herself up and out. She closes the door and watches as Altaf drives away.

Altaf used to help her to the front door, but she made him stop when she saw the neighbours—especially those from the community—staring. They felt sorry for her. She knew it. Poor old lady, living all by herself, when all of them were surrounded by their families—like those old sisters, Dolat and Shahsultan, who had moved in together after their husbands died. This was one of the reasons Tajdin bought in this area. He liked the fact that there were so many Ismaili families close by. This way, he had said to his mother, she would have company when he was at work. Zera had made friends with some of them—even if she really didn't like any of the women. (And she certainly couldn't make friends with any of the men.) All day, these women, they just talked nonsense, gossiping about this one and that one. What is the point of discussing the sorrows of other people's lives? But she tolerated it—for Tajdin's sake.

After Tajdin fell into the coma, Dolat and Shahsultan came around and enquired about his well-being. "If there's anything you need, anything at all, please tell us." Many others called, but soon Zera became exhausted responding to all their queries. She was sure that many were secretly happy that misfortune had fallen on her house, instead of theirs. Eventually, she just ignored the doorbell and stopped answering the phone. Members from the Social Welfare Committee called too, but she said she was fine and didn't need their help.

As Zera walks toward her house, her keys already in her hand, she spots Dolat, standing in front of her living room window with her grandson in her arms. Zera looks away and continues up the walk, her heavy canvas bag hanging from her fingers, only a few inches above the ground.

Inside her house, Zera twists the blinds closed. She has caught many children in the complex shamelessly peering in. She turns on the TV to channel 4, which displays scrolling news text with a weather and time bar at the bottom. (She still has the satellite dish but does not know how to use it. Besides, having so many channels confuses her.) The living room fills with a soft blue glow and elevator music. She spends the next hour getting things ready for tomorrow's orders. Zera has the urge to go to the bathroom, but holds it. She would rather get all her work done first, before relaxing. She removes several packages of meat from the large deep-freezer in the dining room, and places them on a tray on the counter to defrost. She organizes the spices that she requires, then reviews the orders and prepares labels for the Safeway bags. Finally, she allows herself to go to the washroom, where she also changes into her nightgown, which has a dark-yellow turmeric stain over one breast.

Zera returns to the kitchen and warms up a side plate of *kuku paka* in the microwave, and when she's done eating, she washes her plate and teacup with antibacterial dish liquid, then places them upside down on a tea towel next to the sink. She sets her series of alarm clocks, checking each one twice before she takes four pills (the blue one for digestion, the white one to stop the urge to urinate at night, two orange ones for her arthritis), then settles into her bed. She recites her *du'a*, removes her dentures, and finally lies down to sleep. It is five-thirty in the afternoon.

IN THE MORNING, Zera ensures that she is ready earlier than usual. But Altaf, thankfully, does not arrive before the appointed time of 3 A.M. She locks the patio door and walks down the gravel path to the back gate. As she approaches the minibus, Altaf swings open the double doors. "Hey, Ma, why are you limping so much? *Anji*-arthritis-*ai*?" Altaf steps down and offers Zera his arm.

She hands him her canvas bag instead. "*Na-rey-na,* not my arthritis, bheta. Something in my shoe." Zera steadies herself against the door frame and lifts herself into the minibus. Altaf jumps in, and after she has lowered herself into her usual seat on the first row, he kneels down and reaches for her foot.

Zera presses back into her seat. "What are you doing? Paying your respects to an old woman, hanh?" She laughs, her face flushing pink.

"Let me take a look."

"*Arrey,* why you fussing? It's nothing." Zera clucks her tongue. "Forget it now. Let's go, let's go. If we leave your crazy *bhoodhas* waiting outside for too long, they'll have your head."

Altaf shakes his head. "It'll only take a second." He cups her ankle and carefully slips off her running shoe as if it were a glass slipper.

Zera curls her toes like a little girl and looks away.

"Ah-ha!" Altaf peels off a pebble stuck on Zera's support hose, and pinches it between two fingers. "Here's the culprit."

"Give it," Zera says, and when he places it on her palm, she tries to smile as she clenches her hand into a tight fist.

Altaf gets behind the wheel, pushes a tape of *ginans* into its socket, and shifts the bus into drive.

A group of seniors has already gathered at the first designated pick-up point—a roundabout at the entrance to the townhouse complex. The minibus slowly fills up. Zera avoids making eye contact with any of them—especially Dolat and Shahsultan.

"How's it, bheta?" Dolat says as she climbs to the top step, Shahsultan behind her, and hands Altaf a cassette. "Top Hits 1997. My son made it for me. What a good boy I have, hanh? Even has the latest, *Pardes*. Too good, I'm telling you, too good. You have seen it?"

Altaf shakes his head. "I haven't been able to get a copy. Shaz's sold out too quickly."

"Don't you worry, I'll get you one."

Zera unravels the *tasbih* from around her wrist, shuts her eyes, and starts her morning *salwat*.

"No, it's fine, Ma. I'll just wait," Altaf protests.

"No, no! You must see it only. What is the use in waiting, bheta? I'll tell my son first thing."

Altaf turns his palms up. "Okay, I give up. But this time, I'm going to pay for it."

Zera's eyes pop open. Why are these people talking so loudly this early in the morning? I can't even concentrate on my prayers.

"We'll see, we'll see." Dolat cups Altaf's chin in her palm. "How can I take money from you, hanh? Look how much good *seva* you are doing for all of us."

I know exactly what she is trying to imply, Zera thinks. As if I'm a *nindi-gigli,* that I don't understand. Always putting her nose in other people's business. Thinks she knows everything about everybody's life! What the hell does she know about my life? As if I don't pay Altaf for helping me make my deliveries.

From the lower step, Shahsultan pushes at her sister's backside. "*Haya,* get in, Dolly."

Dolat shakes her head. "I'm going, *bana.* Can't even say a proper hello these days or what?" She swats her sister's hand away and walks down the aisle, waving to the other passengers before she lowers herself into her regular seat, behind Zera. Shahsultan climbs in and settles in next to her sister. Good thing, Altaf had once quipped to Zera, that Shahsultan is so skinny; otherwise how would those two ever manage to sit together?

"Why not play Top Hits, Altaf?" Shahsultan asks, coughing into a handkerchief.

A few others from the back pipe in. "Yes, yes."

Altaf obliges. He ejects the *ginan* tape and replaces it with the Hindi film songs.

"Louder, sey!" one of the men at the back yells.

Altaf turns up the volume.

Zera removes her Walkman from her handbag and as she slips on the headphones, she can see Dolat's and Shahsultan's reflections in the window, shaking their heads and snapping their fingers. Always just want to enjoy themselves, these people. If not here, then on their regular seniors' trips organized by Council—

picnics at Bowness Park, card games at Kerby Centre, music parties with bands flown in all the way from Vancouver. What a waste of time and money! Zera hangs her head and tries to concentrate on her prayers—at least, she tells herself, until they arrive at the jamatkhana, where all of them will get off and she will finally have some peace.

Zera is staring out at the rows and rows of unlit houses, which look like shadows that have been erected to standing, when her Walkman suddenly stops. She fumbles with the buttons in the dark. The radio comes on and before she can stop it, the announcer's voice booms into her ear. She reaches up to remove the headphones, but instead her hands stay cupped on her ears, as if in *namaz,* and she is forced to listen to the story: *Diana, Princess of Wales, died early this morning of injuries sustained in a high-speed car crash that also killed her companion and Harrods heir, Dodi Fayed, the French government said. The thirty-six-year-old princess died at four this morning, Paris time.* Zera is not sure why, but she mouths the word *no,* over and over again to herself. A royalty expert joins the radio announcer. The monarchy, she says, was not yet ready for a modern princess—an unconventional woman who refused to be boxed into her role. Zera clasps her hands on her lap and swallows. The expert then begins to recount memorable images from the princess's short life. Diana arriving at St. Paul's Cathedral in her fairy-tale wedding dress, yards of silk trailing behind her; the People's Princess cradling a baby with AIDS; the daring princess, frolicking in London town with her then sister-in-law, the Duchess of York; the mother of the future king running barefoot in a race at her son's school; the Queen of Hearts, a few steps behind her husband's mistress at his polo match; and then the beautiful princess, alone, in front of the greatest monument of love, the Taj Mahal.

Out of nowhere, Zera now feels the pain of the pebble in her clenched fist, biting into her skin. She uncurls her fingers and releases the pebble, the size of a child's tooth. It rolls down the front of her legs and hits the floor with a soft *ting*. It's only when she rubs a finger over the groove left on her palm that she begins to feel something unwind inside of her, like the machinery of a clock, and then suddenly she starts to weep openly in the community minibus—not only for a death that came too soon for a young princess but also for all those who will soon wake from their deep slumber this morning, and learn, at long last, about her story.

ACKNOWLEDGMENTS

My trusted first readers: Karim Ladak, who has the ability to see beauty in everything and without whom this book, among so much else, would have been impossible; and Marguerite Pigeon, who constantly inspires me and who helped shape this book with her astute feedback.

My family, who supported and believed in me, and who eagerly fished for details—not only in their memories but also through a ready network of people across the country. (The phone companies thank you, too.) The expert fishers include my parents, my sister Shemin, and my brothers-in-law Karim (especially for the story "A Christmas Baby"), Arshil, and Imtiaz.

A special thank you to my parents, Nurali and Rozina Mohamedali, who despite their worrying hearts supported me in every way they could.

My sister Tazmina, who is always there for me. Thanks also to her and Karim for regularly providing me with a seat on Makhani Airlines.

My sister Naseem (the Guli to my Budlou), with whom my love for storytelling first began.

My nieces and nephews, who share their worlds with me: Salina, Nadeem, Shahina, Shahir, Alykhan. Hana also because her birth, in many ways, led to the birth of this book.

My friends, near and far, for all their support, especially Kapil Khatter, Rashmi Varma, Vanita Varma, Nep Sidhu, Vanz

Acknowledgments

Chapman, Stany Bergeron, and Kavita Talreja. A special thank you to Elizabeth Bachinsky, Rajinderpal S. Pal, and Marika Deliyannides, who also provided valuable feedback on some stories. Sylvia Eastman for her exacting copy edits on several stories.

At Penguin Canada, David Davidar for his resolute confidence, Barbara Berson for her keen editorial insight, and Tracy Bordian for her flexibility and skill during production.

At UBC's Creative Writing School, Maureen Medved, George McWhirter, and Andreas Schroeder for their guidance in completing the initial draft of the manuscript.

The many people who helped me start this journey, including Aritha van Herk and Rosemary Nixon, and especially Shyam Selvadurai, who encouraged me to "take the plunge" and, when I finally emerged, graciously introduced me to literary agent Nicole Winstanley, about whom not enough can be said.

filling Station and *Event* magazines, where I was first published. Your support has been invaluable. *The Journey Prize Stories* and *Toronto Life* for boosting my confidence early on.

Three books in particular: Mahmood Mamdani's *From Citizen to Refugee*, M.G. Vassanji's *Gunny Sack*, and Ngugi wa Thiong'o's *Petals of Blood*.

Also, Karima Bapoo-Mohamed for her help with historical details that shaped the story "Open House."

The Canada Council for the Arts and the Ontario Arts Council for their generous support.

Although this book is a work of fiction, I often used historical facts to frame a story. If there are any inaccuracies, they are my own.